ANNA SPARROWS

Ted's Temerity

Littles & Lace Book 3

Cover Design by: Ky at Blue Brolli Graphics

First edition

This book was professionally typeset on Reedsy.
Find out more at reedsy.com

Contents

Preface

This is Book 3 of the *Littles & Lace* series, however it can be read as a standalone.

For this novel in particular, please pay close attention to the content warnings in bold.

Please bear in mind that, while this is a low(ish)-angst (no miscommunication!), sweet & cute, instant-attraction romance, this book does contain discussion of **child loss, homophobia, parental pressure, and anxiety.**

Similarly, this book is an MM Age Play/Age Regression romance between consenting adults with **an age gap** (14 years) and includes feminization/femme play/princess play* and **spanking/impact play**. There are also very brief mentions of other characters indulging in ABDL, but there are no scenes of that type in this novel, as Zephyr is more Middle than Little.

I am still a firm believer in not yucking someone else's yum, so if these kinks aren't for you, don't read them.

Life's too short to read something you don't enjoy.

*PS - while I don't believe that toys, clothing, and modes of play should be gendered, I'm using these terms as the generally accepted description for the kink in question

Acknowledgement

This novel was a whole new experience for me. I managed to trigger myself emotionally while exploring Ted's backstory (thanks, Ted), and with how heavy and serious the subject matter is, I wanted to be absolutely certain that I was handling it properly, while still keeping with the sweet & cute, hyper-fluffy storytelling that the *Littles & Lace* series is coming to be known for.

So I did something new. I reached out (anxiously) for beta readers.

Amur and Cindy answered my call. Without these two amazing people, I don't know what I would have done with *Ted's Temerity.*

The feedback and suggestions Amur and Cindy gave me on the first draft helped me shape this book into what you hold in your hands now. They made me a better writer, and I like to think that they've also become my friends over the process. I'm an introvert by nature, socially awkward and a little weird at best, and making new connections only seems to get harder the more I age.

So, from the bottom of my heart, thank you both again for

being brutally honest, constructive, and so wonderfully helpful. I don't think words can properly express just how grateful I am for your help with this one, or how pleased I am to have made such lovely new friends on this unexpected twist on my journey as an author.

Chapter One – Ted

"…To have and to hold from this day forward until death do you part?"

The question is quite solemn, but the officiant delivering them is anything but. The short, curvaceous woman is wearing a bright pink dress and her hair, cut into a spiky pixie style, matches it. She's bubbly and bright and is grinning at my best friend, Charlie, waiting for the guy to answer.

Seeing as I'm Charlie's Best Man, I give him a little nudge. In front of us, our assembled friends chuckle while Charlie clears his throat and finally answers with the only possible words he could. "I do." From where I'm standing, I can see that the sides of his neck and the skin on his jawline and cheeks not covered by his trademark dark stubble are turning a little pink.

The officiant winks at him and teases, "Right answer!"

Everyone laughs at that. Then she turns to Charlie's fiancé and asks the whole spiel again. I can see Asher's entire face from my spot behind Charlie's turned form. The younger man is practically vibrating with joy as he stares across at the man

1

he's marrying. His curly hair has been trimmed and artfully styled, and his hazel eyes are shining brightly under the hot summer sun.

Thank God this is a casual wedding. The grooms are dressed in matching white linen short sleeved shirts and beige khakis. Matt and I, standing for Ash and Charlie respectively, are wearing the same pants, but short sleeved shirts in a pale blue color. It's late afternoon and there's enough of a breeze that we're not sweltering, but I'll be glad when this ceremony's over and we can crack open some crisp, cold bottles of beer.

Ash gives the same answer, the officiant declares them husband and husband, they kiss and we all cheer.

"Congratulations to you both," I drag Charlie in for a hug first, then Asher right after him. "I'm so happy for you."

Charlie pats me on my shoulder blade, but Ash squeezes me tight. "Thanks, Uncle Ted." I resist the urge to ruffle his hair. I can see that effort has gone into styling it today, and probably a bit of product besides. "Next time'll be you, right?"

I snort. I've known Ash for almost as long as he's been with Charlie, which is coming up on three years now. And in that time, while I've gone on a few dates from guys I met at The Grove, the local BDSM club, I haven't found the sort of connection that Ash and Charlie share. Additionally, there's a lot about my past that not even Charlie's aware of which, after close to fifteen years of friendship, would be difficult and painful to explain now. Instead, I focus on the obvious.

"I'm almost fifty," I argue with a shake of my head.

It's a mild exaggeration. I still have a few years before I hit that milestone, but it's sneaking up fast.

At Asher's questioning glance, I sigh. "I think I'm getting too old to believe I'll find someone to settle down with now." I shrug, forcing a bright smile that I hope meets my eyes. "But this is your wedding day, kiddo. Let's not bring down the mood."

Until recently, I was also Ash's boss in addition to being his and Charlie's friend. But he graduated college, having deferred and then studied part time after he met Charlie, and is now working with his husband. Together they're building a community hub for people like us: people in the BDSM lifestyle, with additional focus to those who enjoy the age regression kink. I've been helping out with some of the legalities, but Asher's business degree has proven useful for them, as have Charlie's connections from his previous career as a cop.

I'm significantly older than both of these men, but our social circle is eclectic. That's to be expected, considering we all met through the BDSM lifestyle.

Case in point: Ash's best friend, Matt, wanders over with his Daddy's hand clutched in his. To look at them, you'd assume the roles were reversed. They're both tall, broad men, with Matt eclipsing London in height and muscle mass. Matt's arms are heavily tattooed, and his neatly trimmed beard is more salt and pepper now than the brown it once was. The shaggy hair on his head, also neatly styled back today, is turning the same. He's roughly my age, so that's hardly a surprise. But his Daddy, London, is in his late twenties with thick, black hair and the flawless skin of youth. Like Ash and Charlie, their Daddy-boy relationship has been going strong since they met.

And, alright, if Matt could still find love in his mid-forties, maybe I'll concede that hope is not lost for me after all. It just seems unlikely.

"Congrats, guys," London gives the grooms each a quick hug

before drawing Matt back against his side, "that was a really nice ceremony."

"Yeah, it was," Matt agrees, snuggling against his Daddy's shoulder. His tone is wistful and dreamy. "The weather was perfect, too."

We'd all expressed our concerns that choosing to marry in the park without a backup plan for bad weather was asking for trouble, but Ash held firm. He's quite stubborn when he wants to be.

As if reading my thoughts, he casts me a smug little grin. "Told you it would be."

I shake my head. "You got lucky."

Charlie chuckles at that and tugs his new husband flush against him. "I'd say *I* got lucky," he says, aiming for schmoopy and disgustingly sweet.

Thankfully, his younger brother, Josh, has also meandered over from his spot among the guests. "Nah," he teases, "that's what your wedding night is for, isn't it?" He waggles eyebrows that match Charlie's for emphasis.

Charlie sighs with exasperation when we all snicker like teenagers. He shoots his younger brother a glare. "Fuck off, Josh."

"You wound me," Josh places a hand over his chest, then lunges for Ash. "We're officially brothers now!"

"He gets this from Mom," Charlie tells us as an aside, as though we're not all aware of the fact.

"Speaking of," I jut my chin towards the woman in question.

She's bustling across the manicured lawn like a woman on a mission, practically dragging her husband (an older version of Charlie and Josh) along beside her. Charlie's baby brother, Axel, follows at a more sedate pace. Unlike his older brothers, Axel's short and stocky, with his mother's rounded facial features and curled hair. He graduated high school a couple of years ago, but still looks like a teenager to me. Then there's Charlie's sister, Maisy, and her husband whose name I can't remember. Charlie's family are lovely, but they're high energy and I'm already looking for my escape.

"Ted," Chance, one of the other Daddies in our little group, calls me just as Charlie's mother reaches us. I could kiss him. "Can you come help with the…uh…"

"The cooler," another younger man, one I don't recognize, steps in smoothly.

I try not to swallow my tongue as I look him up and down. I try to gauge his age and guesstimate that he's likely in his early thirties. He's immaculately dressed in a tailored suit (*in this heat? Is he crazy?*), all long limbs and big, dark eyes. He's got the prettiest smile I've ever seen, and his skin is, as Ricky Martin sang about a fictional paramour, the color of mocha. His voice is like liquid velvet, soft and sensual, and I'm too busy listening to the melodic tone to actually focus on the words.

"Sorry," I shake my head as though to clear it, belittling myself for the moment of infatuation. This man is beautiful but, even if he is kink friendly, the likelihood of him being a Little or wanting a Daddy as old as I am is slim to none. Assuming he's even single. "The cooler?"

"Yes," he looks amused, stepping in closer to me. "Can you come help with the cooler? We need to load it into the back of Chance's truck and it's just a bit too heavy for me to help properly." He bats insanely long lashes at me and I nod my agreement readily. Right now, I'd happily follow this pretty little thing anywhere.

My nameless savior apologizes to the grooms and Charlie's

family for stealing me away, then leads me towards the parking lot. Finally getting my shit together, I look around for Chance, who we appear to have left behind.

Ah, well, he'll catch up. Thanks for taking one for the team, Chance.

"He said you'd need rescuing from Charlie's family," my companion tells me, interpreting my confusion correctly. "Unfortunately, it seems Chance isn't so great at improv."

"No, he's not," I agree, then stick my hand out to properly introduce myself. "Thanks for the rescue. I'm Ted."

Full, plump lips twitch upwards before he takes my hand. "Zephyr."

That…well, that was not at all the sort of name I was expecting.

Zephyr laughs. It's a surprisingly deep sound, considering the pitch of his speaking voice. "Yeah," he says, "I get that reaction a lot."

"What?" I try to recover. "I didn't say anything."

"You didn't need to. You had that 'how the hell does this guy have such a white boy hippy name?' look on your face. Don't worry; *everyone* looks at me like that." He shrugs. "My parents *are* hippies, by the way. At least at heart. I mean, Dad's an accountant and Mom's a teacher, but they're still very, uh, *creative*. So…" he gestures loosely over his lithe body, charmingly self-deprecating, "Zephyr it is."

Shoving my hands in my pockets, I rock back on my heels. "For what it's worth, I think it's a pretty cool name."

'Pretty cool'? Am I stuck in the 90s now? Why not just say 'rad' and really prove how lame I am?

Oblivious to my internal cringing, Zephyr smiles again. "Thank you."

Awkward silence begins to descend. I don't want that. "So," I start, fumbling for conversation. I'm not used to fumbling. I'm usually cool as a cucumber. Suave. Sophisticated. "How do you know Chance?"

I want to facepalm as soon as the probing question leaves my lips. I might as well have asked if they're fucking.

Well done, Theodore. Walk away now before you really put your foot in it.

Zephyr, thankfully, throws me a bone. "Actually, I met him and Asher at The Grove." His posture is deliberately relaxed, but I can see him eyeing me for my reaction.

I nod and smile. "Littles' Night? Those are Ash's favorite." And when Charlie can't make it, Spence, Chance or I usually step in as his caregiver. I cock my head, looking Zephyr up and down slowly. "I don't want to assume…"

"Oh, I'm very much a Little." Once again, he takes me out of my misery. He looks me up and down, much the same way I just did to him. It makes me feel better about the exchange, like we're on equal footing. "I'd guess Daddy, but after Chance introduced me to Matt, I also don't want to presume."

"Definitely a Daddy," I nod, trying not to let my excitement over the basic compatibility between us show. Before the silence can descend again, I ask, "Are you new to The Grove?" I haven't visited recently, but I'd definitely remember seeing him around.

"Yeah. New to town, actually. Only been here a few months, and Ash…well, you know Ash." He laughs, shaking his head. "He wouldn't hear of me not coming to the wedding when he worked out how very limited my social circle here is, so…" Zephyr extends his arms out wide, palms facing the clear, blue sky. "Here I am."

I know my expression has turned fond as I think about Ash. He's flourished from the skittish, traumatized kid he was when he first stumbled into Charlie's life. And, because he knows what it's like to be lonely and to start over somewhere new, it's not surprising that he tries to welcome every new face with open arms.

"Well, I'm glad you came today," I find myself telling Zephyr, once again wondering where all of my ability to flirt and charm disappeared to. "And not only because you rescued me from Charlie's family."

It's a clunky save, but it'll do.

"Oh, is that so?" Zephyr practically purrs, stepping in a little closer. His dark eyes practically dance with amusement. "Why else would you be glad that I, a complete stranger to you, am here, then?"

Good question.

Before I can fumble over an answer that doesn't sound creepy as fuck, Chance interrupts us, throwing his arm around my shoulder while he grins at Zephyr. Chance's enthusiasm is usually infectious, innocuous as he is with his dad bod and ginger beard, but today the interruption grates on my nerves.

"Mission accomplished," he declares, sounding proud of himself. "Now all we gotta do is try and sit at the far end of the table at the fancy-schmancy restaurant you booked for tonight, and we can avoid Mrs Walker trying to marry us all off."

Honestly, considering the casual attire of the Wedding Party, it's not like we're going anywhere that exclusive, but I don't bother arguing with my friend. Instead, I allow his comment to launch us into a debate about the merits of getting to the restaurant early vs late, and I'm thrilled beyond measure when

Zephyr agrees to ride with us in Chance's truck when we finally get our shit together and leave the park.

Chapter Two — Zephyr

"So...Ted, huh?" Ash asks, dropping into the chair beside me at his very casual wedding reception.

It turned out, as his gift to his friends, one Theodore Masters hired a private room at their favorite restaurant. How do I know this? Asher and his new husband, Charlie, were sure to thank the man effusively during their impromptu speeches as we ate. Sitting beside me, the very same man tried to brush off the thanks casually, but I could tell he was genuinely happy to have been able to help his friends out.

I haven't known Ash very long, and this is only the third time I've met Charlie, but they're good people.

Well, good...if somewhat nosy.

I do my best to appear unaffected by my new friend's observational skills. "What about him?" I ask nonchalantly, reaching for the glass of sweet white wine I've been nursing for the last half hour. I'm not a big drinker, but I do have a weakness for sweet things.

The room we're in is just long enough for the extended table

"

which seats twenty people. Ash and Charlie had taken seats next to each other in the middle, with Charlie's family down one end and his and Ash's friends clustered on the other. I found myself seated among their friends, which was nice.

It's actually a lovely space. The room is cozy and warmly lit, the walls painted cream. Fairy lights are strung above our heads. There's a small, makeshift 'dance floor' in the other half of the room, and now that dinner is over, some of the couples in attendance are swaying together to the strains of Michael Bublé's crooning.

Charlie's being begrudgingly dragged around the dance space by his mother, but when he looks over at Ash in an obvious cry for help, my new friend just giggles and blows his husband a kiss. Then he turns back to me and raises an eyebrow. "Oh, nothing," he answers my question with airy amusement, "just the fact that you've been eyeing him off all night."

I shrug. "He's an attractive man."

Ted is tall and broad shouldered, with dark brown hair and a healthy tan. He has salt and pepper streaks at his temples and artfully scattered atop his head, which seems almost artificial considering the way they perfect his silver fox vibe. A strong, clean-shaven jawline and warm light brown eyes round out the image. His voice isn't ridiculously deep, but it's smooth and measured when he speaks, likely a byproduct of his chosen career as a lawyer.

Ash's smirk turns knowing. "Uh huh. And he's an excellent Daddy."

I don't bother reacting to that, either. I'd gathered as much just from our interactions alone. When we arrived at the restaurant and took our seats, Ted slid into the one beside mine, and it seemed almost second nature for him to look after me for the course of the meal, refilling my glass, checking that things were to my liking, being sure to include me in the conversations he fell into with the people around us. I guess that, if he'd been given the chance, he would have even cut my steak for me.

After the meal, he'd been dragged into conversation with someone at the far end of the table and I'd encouraged him to go chat. I knew Chance as well, after all, and even if I do come off shy, I can socialize with strangers without any issues. But Ash was right when he said I'd been eyeing Ted all night: even with him on the far side of the room, my eyes still stray to him.

"Does your new husband know that you're trying to play matchmaker for his best friend?" I tease lightly, leaning back in my chair to stretch off the soporific effects of the decadent meal I just ate.

"Yep," Ash pops the 'p' as he speaks the word with childlike glee. "And he's all for it. Ted's been single for too long, and, honestly, we both just wanna see him happy."

"Maybe there's a reason Ted's been single," I argue, then hold up a finger to defend my point when it's clear Ash is unimpressed at the implication that his friend is somehow flawed. "And I don't mean that he's not a good guy, because it's obvious that he is. Just…maybe he *wants* to be single. Maybe he's the type that likes to hit it and quit it."

Ash scoffs. "He's a *Daddy*," he tells me in a tone that says I'm being stupid. "He has dedicated space for age regression play in his home *and* in his office." That last tidbit does surprise me, and I know it shows on my face. Ash's vehemence gentles. "Apparently, he'd just come out of a long-term relationship around the time I met Charlie. He's been on a few dates here and there, but he hasn't really clicked with anyone." Now, an almost lupine grin pulls his lips upwards. "Until now."

I roll my eyes. "And what would you know of our interactions, hmm? It's your wedding day. You've been too loved up with that handsome man of yours to be paying little ol' me any mind."

"*Please.* People watching is something Charlie and I both enjoy." There's a sharpness to Ash's grin now: a hint that he can read me better than I'd like him to be able to. "And, let me tell you, watching the man I like to think of as 'Uncle Ted' fall all over himself to keep your attention was a revelation."

I take a moment to process those words, patting the corners of my mouth delicately with my thick, white linen napkin before tossing it over the crumbed remnants of my slice of wedding cake. "Alright, so there was a *little bit* of flirting…" I hold my thumb and index finger an inch or so apart. "But it's a wedding. Don't all single people get a bit flirty with all the happily ever after vibes going on?" Not to mention the alcohol, not that I've had more than two glasses.

"You weren't flirting with Chance or Spence, though, and they're both single." Ash lets his gaze float around the room, pointing people out. "So's Max, actually." He cocks his head and muses, "I mean, I think he's straight? I don't know. He's Charlie's former partner. Anyway, I know Tristan and Gabe are single, and they're involved in the BDSM lifestyle, too." He waves at the two men he just named when they look over. Both are, objectively speaking, handsome men. Probably too young for my taste, but with pleasant smiles and friendly eyes. "They're also new friends of ours," he adds, offhandedly. "We met them through Cherie and Kate. Tristan's a counselor and Gabe's a social worker. They're helping with the community center." He shrugs. "Not sure what their kinks are, but they're involved in the lifestyle, too."

I nod, but my disinterest in any of the men he just mentioned is almost palpable. "Okay, fine, you've made your point," I laugh, shaking my head before my gaze once again seeks out Ted. He's currently leaning against the far wall with a beer in hand, apparently engrossed in casual conversation with the woman Ash introduced earlier as Cherie, as well as his friends Matt and London. As I watch him, I can feel Ash studying me. I sigh. "What do you suggest I do about it, then?"

It's not like I'm going to actually take Ash's advice on board. I'll humor him. I'll listen and pretend to think it over, and then I'll slink out the door alone as planned.

Don't get me wrong: I like Ted. I like him a lot. And I don't doubt that he'd make a fantastic Daddy for someone. But…I'm not exactly a 'traditional' Little and, as much as I can tell Ted finds me attractive, I don't know that our role-playing tastes would match. From what I've gathered just from listening to Ash talk about his circle of friends, someone like Ash himself is more Ted's type. A perfect little boy.

Not someone like me.

See, I'm Little, but I like to play dress ups. Princess style.

Now, I know there's absolutely nothing wrong with that. I'm not ashamed to literally wear my kink with pride. However, I also know that finding a Daddy whose interests match mine can be difficult. Tea parties vs train sets, you know? And that's fine. I'm not desperate to find a Daddy just yet. I'm happy to have my itches scratched at The Grove for now.

Besides, I'm only slowly getting back into the lifestyle after an unscheduled break from it. Am I ready to dive in so deeply with a handsome stranger just because we've gotten along for one meal?

"Ask him to dance?" Ash suggests with a waggle of his eyebrows, bringing my thoughts back to the moment at hand. He grins. "You did tell him you're a professional dancer, didn't you?"

"Was," I correct him, doing my best not to sound bitter about it. A torn ACL ruined my dreams of continued touring. Now I teach dance to grade-schoolers.

I love my job, and I'm glad I recovered enough that I still get to dance, but the life I'm leading now has nothing on the fast pace of touring the world as a backup dancer, or the rush of performing in front of a huge audience. Hell, even being in the chorus line of a musical theater production would be awesome right now. But I had my chance, and I can't complain too much about my lot in life now. I'm not unhappy. I just miss what I once had.

"You're teaching it and that's a profession," he argues with me, oblivious to my inner turmoil, "ergo, you're a professional dancer."

"I should have guessed." Ted's sinfully smooth voice startles me and I jump in my seat, feeling heat rise to my cheeks even though the color of my skin is forgiving of my blushes. I turn to find him standing behind me and Ash, smirking. But, instead of saying something tacky about my body being 'built' like a dancer's, he says, "You're naturally graceful. Your movements are all purposeful, and your posture screams 'dancer'."

Part of me wants to slump in my seat if only out of petulance, but I remain upright with my back straight, my shoulders back and my chin high. "Is that so?"

Ted nods. "If I had to hazard a guess, I'd say you practiced as a ballerino, but..." he cocks his head, as though he's carefully deliberating his choices. He probably is. "No. Ballroom. Am I right?"

My jaw drops. "Yeah, I came up in the world of competitive ballroom dancing. What gave it away?"

"Honestly?"

I arch an eyebrow. "No. Please lie to me."

Ash snickers, then pushes out of the seat he'd commandeered, declaring that his work here is done. I wave him off, my eyes still tracking Ted as he slips into the seat, offering me a slightly bashful look. "Chance showed me your business page. It says it in your bio."

A burst of laughter escapes me. "You Googled me?"

"No," Ted's cheeks are taking on a distinctly pink flush. "Chance did."

"Uh huh."

With a put-upon groan, Ted runs his fingers through his hair. "He *did!*" he insists, then adds, "They're all trying to play matchmaker. They're worse than a bunch of meddling old women." There's a brief pause and he softens his tone. "I apologize if that makes you uncomfortable. They all mean well. But, with two of the guys paired off, Chance and Spence are trying to throw the heat off themselves and—"

"And the couples just want to see y'all as happy as they are." I finish for him, patting his thigh consolingly. "Don't worry. Weddings bring this out in people."

There's a spark of hunger in his gaze, which he directs down to my hand fleetingly. I slowly pull it back into my own bubble of personal space. Ted grins. "I can't be mad at them," he tells me. "It's not like I'm not interested in you."

Oh, but I do like how direct he is. It seems far more mature than half the guys I've dated – men closer to my own age and not involved in the BDSM lifestyle. With all the touring I was doing, I found beggars could not be choosers.

Still, even though Ted *is* a Daddy, and he knows I'm a Little, he doesn't know that I'm into princess play and that's a problem.

Instead of focusing on that, though, my traitorous mouth runs before my brain can do damage control. "Well, good. Because I'm interested in you, too."

Zephyr Cruze, I tell myself as I watch my companion's eyes light up, *quit while you're ahead.*

Chapter Three — Ted

Zephyr and I spend the rest of the party casually getting to know one another. We cover all the easy topics: nothing deep or of much consequence. I learn that he hates bananas but loves strawberries, and I share my firm belief that pineapple has no place on pizza (and he disagrees, calling me a heathen). I discover that we're both dog people, but neither of us hate cats, and it turns out that he shares my enjoyment for old Western movies. He loves musicals, which is not a surprise to me, but I am surprised when he vehemently states that he can't stand most Andrew Lloyd Webber classics.

"So, no *Phantom of the Opera* for you?" I tease.

He makes a face and shakes his head. "Ugh. No. And no *Cats*, either, thanks."

"Fair enough," I reply with a laugh. "I'm more into contemporary musical theater anyway. *Wicked. Avenue Q. The Book of Mormon.* That sort of thing."

Zephyr nods, genuinely invested in the conversation. His dark eyes sparkle under the fairy lights strung overhead and he leans in closer. *"Hamilton?"*

"Also excellent. As was the Broadway version of *In The Heights* but I can't say I loved the film adaptation as much."

He claps his hands with excitement. "Oh! I agree! I mean, the cast was fantastic, but I just couldn't get into it. I can't pinpoint why. It just didn't hit right."

When his face falls with unexpected melancholy, I lean in and reach for his hand. "What's wrong?"

Zephyr gives himself a shake and pastes on a smile that doesn't reach his eyes. "Nothing."

"No," I press, squeezing his hand, thrilled that he allows the contact to continue. "What's wrong?"

I watch him lick his lips, obviously deliberating over the concept of letting me in, even just a little bit. Not that I can blame him: I'm a veritable stranger. But my instincts have me determined to comfort and help him.

"I just…" he exhales. "I miss it. Dancing professionally, I mean." At my questioning glance, he shrugs. "I tore my ACL eighteen months ago. The surgery went well, and my recovery has been good, but my knee never fully recovered. I can dance, but not at the same level I used to, and not for as long or as intensely. It's been a bitter pill to swallow, I guess."

My heart goes out to him. After hearing him talk about his love of dance and music, I can only imagine how deeply this change of circumstances must hurt him. With his hand still in mine, I give him another reassuring squeeze. "I'm so sorry," I tell him.

Charlie went through something similar after the wound to his thigh ended his career, but I never felt like I had the right words to comfort him then, and I don't have them now for Zephyr, either.

"It could be worse," Zephyr says, and it sounds as though it's a mantra he tells himself a lot.

"It could," I find myself agreeing, "but that doesn't mean you can't mourn what you lost."

Shaking his head, he gestures around the room. Half the guests have left by now, but I've resolved to stay put until this charming man leaves first, unwilling to miss even a second of possible conversation with him. "We're at a wedding. It's like a rule to not talk about sad shit, or something."

"You can talk about whatever you want," I argue. "I won't judge."

I've got my own fair share of sad thoughts, after all, but no reason to bring them up. Not now, not ever. Is that healthy? Probably not. But there's no place for them here. Especially not in the company I'm keeping right now.

"Zero judgment, huh?" Zephyr's tone shifts into an attempt at being flirtatious. He bats long, dark lashes at me. "That's a very open promise, Mister Masters."

"I'm *very* open minded, Mister Cruze," I flirt back, deliberately dipping my voice low.

I watch as my Daddy voice registers with him, sending a visible shiver through his lithe frame. I want so badly to make this beautiful man mine. My tiny dancer, to borrow a nickname from Elton John. But I know better than to rush into things. I've made that mistake too often in my lifetime.

There's an interesting gleam in his eyes, something in his expression that hints at him wanting to test me on my playful words, but he blinks it away and says, "I do like the sound of that." Then he raises his left wrist, twisting it to check the time on his watch, and sighs heavily. "And, on that note, I should probably get going. I have early classes tomorrow."

My stomach sinks, but I don't want to come off clingy or too aggressive, so I nod and rise from my seat at the same time as him. "Do you want to share a Lyft?" When he raises his eyebrows, I realize my mistake. I want to smack myself upside the head. Sheepishly, I explain, "I meant to our respective destinations. Not...I wasn't..."

Excellent. I'm back to being a fumbling buffoon.

As frustrated as I am with myself, it's also a sign that I genuinely like this man: that I'm feeling the kind of interest that has evaded me for years now. I can't be mad about that. Even if I do wish I could prevent embarrassing myself quite as badly.

"I should hope not," Zephyr's lip curls upwards and he leans in, his breath ghosting over my ear as he murmurs, "I'd like to be taken on a real date before we start talking about going home together."

He is so close that I can feel the heat of his body next to mine, and the combination of his proximity and those words has me hardening instantly. The knowing expression on his face as he pulls back, putting space between us again, tells me that he's more than aware of the effect he has on people.

On me.

"You're a naughty little thing, aren't you?" I ask, unable to prevent the train of thought that follows my observation.

Is he a bratty boy? Is he into sexual punishments? How far does he push things? How far can I push him back?

"Hmm," he pretends to think about it, and I'm delighted that he's playing along. "Maybe you should give me your number so you can find out for yourself?"

Once again, I can't help but find his confidence insanely alluring. It's a far cry from the shy, sweet Littles I'm used to pursuing, and I'm pulling out my phone before my brain can even catch up. "Give me yours," I insist, "and I'll call you so you'll have mine." I'm not taking any chances here. I can't risk giving him my number without getting his in exchange.

Obviously, if he were to decide that he's not interested, I'd stop pursuing him (no means no, after all), but I'd like to make sure we're on equal footing to begin with. If I don't hear from him in the next few days, I'll reach out. If he turns me down after that? At least I've enjoyed his company tonight and have proven that there's still a chance for me to find someone to connect with after all, even if it doesn't turn out to be him.

As if he's reading my thoughts, he chuckles but rattles off his digits and I type them into my phone. I press the little green handset icon on my screen, and his pocket buzzes with the tell-tale vibration of a silenced phone.

"There," I say, terminating my call. "Now we've got each other's numbers." Still holding my phone, I give it a little shake. "So, want to share a Lyft?"

* * *

Three days. I wait three whole days before I give in to the urge to contact Zephyr. Sitting in my office overlooking a good part of the city, I bring up his contact and press call. It rings for a little while, and I realize that he's probably teaching, but by the time my brain kicks into gear with that thought, I'm being prompted to leave a voicemail message.

"Hi Zephyr, it's Ted. From the wedding. Uh, Ash and Charlie's wedding." Once again, I can feel how awkward I'm being and want to strangle myself for it. I make a living by knowing exactly how best to wield and manipulate the English language. Contract law is my specialty, and I can schmooze potential clients with the best of them. But, apparently, put an attractive man whose kinks complement mine in front of me (or on the phone to me) and I lose all my carefully cultivated skills. "I'm just…touching base." *Ugh.* "And wondering if you might like to go out with me some time?" *Dear God, did my voice just go up half an octave?* I clear my throat. "Give me a call back and we'll chat." *And there I go, over-correcting. What the hell, Masters?* "Talk soon!"

I force myself to hang up before I can humiliate myself further. Staring in horror at the phone in my hand, I ask, "What the ever-loving fuck was that? *'Talk soon!'*" I mock myself in a falsetto, then rub my other palm over my face, cringing at my own behavior. "You're forty-seven. Get it together."

Am I really so out of practice when it comes to wooing a potential partner? It's not like I've been a monk these last three years, but they've been Grindr hookups or guys I've met at The Grove who were flagging for open play. I haven't exactly had to work for another man's attention recently and it shows in my lack of game.

Case in point? I just called it 'game'.

Shoot. Me. Now.

The landline phone on my desk bleats with the tone set for the firm's secretary, thankfully distracting me from my self-deprecating thoughts. I lift the receiver and say, "Yes, Sonya?"

She's a consummate professional, but her voice is always ridiculously chipper. This conversation proves to be no exception. "Your eleven o'clock candidate is here. I've taken the initiative to have him wait in the boardroom for you and Louise."

I glance at my watch, pleased to see that it's only ten to

eleven. A good sign for this candidate. Early, but not stupidly so. "Fantastic, Sonya, thanks."

We're still interviewing for Asher's replacement. Technically, we'd hired someone when he first gave notice, but to say that didn't work out is an understatement. Louise (our Office Manager) and I still grumble over being so thoroughly wrong about our assessment of the guy at the time, the both of us usually priding ourselves on our abilities to read people. Now, with the two of us questioning our judgment, we're probably taking too much time interviewing for the entry-level role, but it's definitely a case of 'once bitten, twice shy'.

"Are you sure we can't just bribe Ash to come back?" Louise jokes when we meet in the hallway outside the conference room. Her long brown hair is secured in an immaculate bun at the back of her head, and her hazel eyes twinkle with mirth as she asks the question. "Aren't you BFFs with his hubby? Surely that gives you some pull."

"It's that same hubby who lured him away from us," I remind her with a put-upon sigh. "Charlie clearly has zero respect for my professional needs."

When I'd been invited to come and meet my best friend's new boy, it had come as quite the surprise to see my most recent hire of the time at Charlie's home. (And I know it had been even more shocking from Asher's perspective; something we can laugh about now.) After that, it took a little while to convince Ash that our professional relationship would be fine, and that I was, first and foremost, Charlie's friend and therefore his friend, too. The fact that he eventually came to think of me as Uncle Ted was both a relief and a privilege.

However, Louise isn't aware of the lifestyle Ash, Charlie and I are involved in. Still, she knows that our friendship is closer than most, and she's convinced that I should be able to use that to my advantage to entice her favorite employee back.

She huffs. "Well, what good is your friendship, then?"

"Aww, come on now, Lou," I cajole, laughter coloring my tone, "we might find someone just as good as Ash." I look down at the completed application and resume in my hand. "Beckett Peters," I read the candidate's name, "might be the one."

With deep resignation, Louise nods. "Fine. But if we don't find a suitable replacement soon? I'm kidnapping Ash back and you can't warn Charlie."

I reach for the door handle and wink. "Let's hope it doesn't have to come to that."

* * *

My phone rings just as I slump through the door from my garage into my empty house. The place is ridiculously big for just me, but I bought it for a song a couple of years ago and have only recently finished the restorations and renovations, bringing it into modern times while keeping its stately feel. I fish my phone out of my pocket, fully prepared to let the call go through to voicemail, when I catch the name on the screen.

Zephyr.

I can't answer it quickly enough, my thumb fumbling for the button.

Thankfully, I manage to catch it before he's redirected to my voicemail, and I know my voice is strained when I answer, "Zephyr! Hello!"

There's a moment of silence, which I interpret as hesitation. "Is this a bad time?"

"No!" I close my eyes and curse myself for the rushed, far-too-eager response. After taking a calming breath, I try again. "No. Sorry. I just got home and had to fumble for my phone."

Great. Verbal diarrhea.

What is it about this man that pulls this from me?

His delicious chuckle floats down the line. "I'm picturing it now," he teases.

Finally, something I can work with. Lowering my voice, I flirt back on my way through the large laundry, passing the equally huge kitchen and into the open plan living/dining space beyond, "Well, I do like that you're picturing me."

Zephyr snorts. "Not in the way you're hoping."

Brat. This sends a thrill up my spine. I'd love to take him over my lap and spank him for his cheek. I get the feeling he'd enjoy it. Even though I've never really been into bratty boys, I know I would as well.

"It's still a step above you *not* thinking of me, so I'll take it."

"Hmm," he makes a show of sounding thoughtful, "If your voicemail is to be taken into consideration, I'm almost certain it's *you* thinking of *me*, Mister Masters."

He's quick as a whip and I love it. Dropping down onto my white leather couch, I lean back and grin at the ceiling with my phone still pressed to my ear. "You called me back, so I can't help but think it's a two-way street, Mister Cruze." Without giving him a chance to respond, I continue, "And I'm not ashamed to admit that I haven't been able to stop thinking about you, if that helps."

"Well, now you've taken all the fun out of my teasing you." I can still hear the smile in his voice, so I know he's not offended.

I want to tell him that I can think of other ways he can tease me and that I'm happy to offer suggestions, but I stop myself.

I want whatever is building between us to be more than just a quick, lusty affair. I'm a Daddy, after all. I'm driven to nurture and care for my partner, which usually involves developing an emotional attachment. Something deeper than just a handful of quick fucks. Not that there's anything inherently wrong with the casual hookups I've had over the last few years, but my heart wants more.

Still, I can't stop myself entirely from flirting back. "Tiny dancer, you can tease me however you like."

A few more beats of silence pass and I pull the phone away, glancing at the screen to make sure the call is still engaged and that I haven't muted it or something similar. When I press it against my ear again, he breathes, "Tiny dancer, huh?"

"You know…like the song?" Suddenly, I feel unsure of myself again, realizing that I've overstepped. Trying to bring back the levity, I blurt, "Or is that well and truly before your time?"

Great. Remind him that there's a massive age gap between you. Idiot.

Thankfully, Zephyr laughs and feigns affront, "I know my Elton John, thank you."

"That's a relief," I sass back, sinking back into the couch cushion now that the crisis has been averted. "Giving you a proper musical education would have become my top priority."

"As opposed to…?"

"As opposed to the date I asked you out on. Which, I might remind you, you still haven't accepted."

"Maybe I was waiting for you to ask again properly, not just via a vague voicemail message."

This beautiful creature is definitely going to keep me on my toes. Smiling, I reply, "Can I take you out to dinner and a movie, Zephyr?"

"How very traditional of you."

Oh, he's really making me work for it.

"Or, perhaps, something more casual? Like a picnic date?" There's a voice in my head telling me not to push too hard. I rack my brain for more creative ideas but, as is becoming the norm where this man is concerned, I can't think beyond just wanting to spend time with him. "Or…bowling?"

Bowling? Really? Who even am I?

"I'd love to go out with you," he finally cuts in, preventing me from spiraling into a list of random activities. But his next words cool my elation, especially with the undercurrent of uncertainty in his voice. "But you should know some things about me, first."

God, I wish that I could see his face. That I could hold his hand as I assure him: "Whatever it is, I doubt it will change my interest in you." Grinning, I try to lighten the mood again. "Even if you tell me that you secretly hate Elton John's music."

This earns me the desired reaction of snorted laughter before a light sigh comes across the line. "I'm a Little, which you know, but…" He trails off.

"But?"

"I'm a femme Little. I'm into princess play and dresses and stuff." Zephyr's voice is small, as though the admission pains him. There are a thousand reasons why that might be the case, but if one of those is that he's afraid I'm not okay with it, I need to disabuse him of that notion right now.

"Is that it?" Okay, probably not the smoothest reaction I could have offered him. I rush to correct myself. "I mean, that's not a problem for me. It doesn't change my interest in you, in general or as a Daddy."

I can hear the breath he sucks in and the wonder in his voice.

"Really?"

"Really." In fact, the whole concept has a feeling of excitement building beneath my skin. I haven't been with a Little who indulged in such things in over a decade, but it's not something I have zero experience with, either. Additionally, Ash has spent the last couple of years re-introducing me to the joys of teddy bear tea-parties. Besides, the whole concept suits Zephyr. The idea of pretty dresses and tea parties and makeup play just fits. I can picture it clearly in my mind's eye, and I love it.

Softening my tone, I hope to impart some of what I'm feeling, "It sounds perfect for you, tiny dancer, and I'd love to be a part of that, if you'll have me."

Chapter Four – Zephyr

I had absolutely no reason to deny Ted when he asked me out a third time. Not after he so sweetly reassured me that my additional kink wasn't an issue for him. The relief I felt in that moment surprised me; I honestly hadn't realized how attached I already was to the idea of dating him until I thought that he might actually change his mind.

So, when he followed up his declaration that he was still into me with another idea for a date, I readily agreed. Even though he changed it from going out to something that sounded far more intimate and personal: dinner at his house, with the potential for some Daddy/Little play if we're both feeling it.

That was on Tuesday. Today is Saturday and the day we'd agreed for our date, and even though we've spent the rest of the week texting during the day and talking on the phone at night, the pre-date jitters are starting to kick in for me.

It's been a week since we met. Somehow, that simultaneously feels like no time at all and far too long. Our conversations have been fun and flirtatious, easy, and effortless. We've talked about everything and nothing. In the lead-up to tonight's date, we spent last night talking about our hard limits as Daddy and Little, and we went through the negotiation chat that really should happen before any BDSM interaction begins.

Considering Ted's experience in the lifestyle, I shouldn't have been surprised that his hard limits are few and far between. He's not into bondage at all but doesn't mind light impact play for fun. As for diapering, he's okay with wetting but draws the line at anything beyond that, which is beyond fine by me. Most of my Little time is spent hovering at a slightly older mindset, so I guess I'm not opposed to being called a Middle, either. Whatever label you put on it, I'm much more interested in pretending I'm a princess than being babied, and I prefer pretty panties to diapers anyway. On the off chance I might wear them, I don't do wetting. Ever. Additionally, pacifiers and bottles don't do it for me at all, and Ted didn't seem upset by that, either.

So far, it sounds like we might actually be well suited to each other, at least where our kinks are concerned.

Yet, I'm nervous. I don't want to screw this up. I actually like this guy.

It's been a while since I've felt so intensely about another man. Before my injury, my affairs were casual at best. It's hard to find Daddies when you're touring, the tight quarters and constant presence of the same people day-in, day-out not helping much. Neither do the hours you have to keep, especially between rehearsals and performances and actually being on the road. Then, after my injury, I went through a dark period, where age play wasn't even on my radar. I just wanted to get off and go home, and I didn't care with whom or in what order of events that happened.

My return to the BDSM scene has been tentative and slow. The night I met Ash and Chance, I was wearing a fairly standard outfit for a Little boy, not giving anyone any inkling about my desires to dress up in pretty dresses or play tea-parties, just dipping my toes back in to the world I'd left behind during the worst year and a half of my life. In fact, tonight will be the first time since my injury that I'm even considering trying.

It hits me that maybe that's a big part of why I feel so anxious.

What if I put on one of my old dresses and don't feel the same way that I used to? I used to feel pretty, and delicate, and magical. What if tonight all I feel is silly? What if that spark is gone? It's been such a big part of who I am for so long, I'm terrified of what it might mean if I've lost it. If I've changed irrevocably.

When Ted picks me up because he insisted on doing so, he gives me a hug in greeting. Then he seems to pick up on my inner turmoil immediately.

"What's wrong?" he asks, gently tilting my head to look me in the eye. "Is going to my place too much, too soon? I'm happy to change our plans if you'd rather something more public and casual."

There's something in the almost rushed way he speaks that has me blinking in surprise. With a jolt, I realize that he's nervous, too. Immediately, some of the tension I've been feeling fades away. His nerves are a sign that he's interested in me for more than just a quick fuck, right? *Right.*

I shake my head, then impulsively step forward and crane my neck to kiss him on the cheek. "You're sweet," I tell him, grinning at the way his cheeks pink from the praise, "and, no, it's not too much or too fast for me."

It's not like we're *planning* on sleeping together yet. We're just planning on testing our compatibility. But I won't complain if that happens to develop into more. Not if we're both on the same page, anyway. I know how quickly BDSM interactions can become intense. How unexpectedly relationships can turn serious simply because of how vulnerable you are being with each other.

"Then what's wrong?" He's a bit like a dog with a bone. I shouldn't be surprised, not with his chosen career. He picks up the overnight bag I packed, which is full of my Little gear, and sets it on the back seat of his BMW.

Because *of course* he drives a BMW.

I sigh and come clean. "I haven't indulged in any of the femme play since before my injury." Licking my lips, I consider my explanation. "I'm just a bit anxious about it. Like…what if I don't feel the same way anymore? It's probably stupid to worry, but if I've been able to just, I don't know, shut it off for the last eighteen months, is it even still part of my identity?"

"Hey now," Ted pulls me in for a hug, carding his fingers through my hair. With my ear pressed to his chest, the steady beating of his heart calms my jangled nerves. "It sounds like you haven't really had enough time to properly explore your kinks at all, let alone since your accident. The fact that you still think about and still have the urge to do it says more about how much you enjoy it than you're aware."

I'm only half processing his words, too swept up in the feeling of being wrapped in his embrace. His chest is warm and solid, and he smells so good. His cologne is sweet and subtle, soothing in its own right. Then there's his voice, pitched low and smooth, rumbling through his chest beneath my cheek and ear. All combined, I feel overwhelmingly safe in his arms. Cared for.

He's not the first Daddy to have ever held me, but I can't recall another Daddy ever making me feel this way. At least, not without the additional post-orgasm endorphins to help.

I try to shoo away the path that thought wants to take me down, but it's too late. I'm immediately wondering how it might feel to be cradled against Ted's body in the afterglow of sex.

Thankfully, he distracts me before I can get too lost in those ponderings. Giving me a little shake, he asks, "Zephyr? Are you okay?"

He sounds genuinely concerned and I reluctantly step back so I can smile at him and nod. "I was just enjoying the hug. It's, uh, it's been a while."

Wow, that sounds pathetic.

But there's no pity in his expression. Instead, he offers me a rueful smile of his own. "I can relate to that."

Well done, Z. First rule of dating: don't bring the mood down. And what did you do? You brought the mood down.

Rallying, I try to turn it around. "Well, if all goes well, maybe we'll both be seeing more hugs in the near future."

It's an awkward attempt, but the blinding smile it earns me tells me that the sentiment is appreciated anyway.

"I hope so," Ted says, and the smile melts into something a little more sensual. "I think we'll be good for each other in a lot of ways."

I'm pretty much convinced that we will, too.

* * *

"I'm sorry, I thought you said you were taking me to your *house*," I blurt with what is probably a slack-jawed, wide-eyed look on my face as Ted pulls his car into the driveway of something I'd otherwise describe as a McMansion. "This," I gesture towards the stately building, "is not a 'house', Ted." I use my fingers as quotation marks while I emphasize how badly his blasé description failed him. "This is a mansion."

It actually takes my breath away to look up at it as the car crawls through the gate towards it. The pretty dappled brickwork is complemented by pristine arch-shaped windows trimmed in white. It's only two stories, but the building sprawls sideways, with at least eight windows that I can count on the ground floor and six on the 'smaller' floor on top of it. Ted presses a button on the little remote attached to his sun visor and the white double garage door on the right side of the home begins to rise slowly.

Finally responding to my reaction to his not-so-humble abode, my date chuckles. "It's not a mansion. It's just a large house."

"You keep telling yourself that," I insist as he directs the car into the spare space in his garage, next to a gleaming Harley Davidson motorcycle. It looks like a cruiser? Honestly, I know nothing about the things. I eye the black and chrome beast with additional surprise before shaking my head. "I wasn't expecting that, either."

"Oh, the bike?" He shrugs. "Let's call that a midlife crisis."

"You don't ride it much?"

Shutting off the car, Ted unbuckles his belt and sighs. "Not as often as I thought I would."

I could throw statistics at him about how dangerous it is to ride them, but I save my breath. He doesn't strike me as the type to make risky decisions on the road, and there's no way to control other road users. I could just as easily be mowed down at a crosswalk as his bike could be hit by an inattentive driver. Instead, I make a vague noise of commiseration and then allow him to guide me through the internal door from the garage into a comically large laundry, with a long marble bench running the length of the space on one side, and gleaming appliances and a massive laundry tub on the other.

"Your laundry is bigger than my bathroom and kitchen combined," I mutter with only a little exaggeration.

He calls me out on it, his tone amused. "That sounds like hyperbole to me."

Before I can dig my heels in and argue that it's really not, he takes my hand and pulls me forward. We exit the laundry into a wide hallway-like space, then pass his kitchen (which, I tease, has to be at least twice the size of my bedroom) and an open plan living-dining area.

The floors throughout are gleaming dark timber, but the walls are off-white, and the counters are all topped with the same light-colored marble as those in the laundry. In the kitchen, the cupboards are the same off-white as the walls, beveled like the garage door. The furniture across all the rooms is all white as well, which contrasts spectacularly with the dark timber flooring, making the whole place feel even bigger and brighter.

Overall, it's a fabulous mix of modern and classic design, and I feel both comfortable and wholly out of place.

"There's also a formal lounge and formal dining room down here," Ted says as he continues to give me the tour, oblivious to my growing unease at the juxtaposition between his world and mine, "and a small office. Upstairs," we've stopped in the main foyer, heralded by a massive double door painted white and a grand staircase carpeted in off-white, with wrought-iron banisters curling up towards the second floor, "there are four bedrooms. Two of those are proper suites —the master and the guest— and the other two standard. Those two share a bathroom." He smiles at me. "The one closest to the master is the playroom."

"This is…" Too much. Too ostentatious. Too insane to even imagine. "*Wow.*"

I knew that, as a senior partner at law firm which, according to Google, is a pretty successful and sought-after one at that, Ted wasn't exactly lower-middle class like me, but this level of wealth makes me uncomfortable.

I mean, I'm a performer. From when I left home at eighteen and into my early twenties, I was literally a starving artist, one missed paycheck away from homelessness. Things got better when I started booking contracts to tour as a backup dancer, but I still had to watch my spending. Then, after injuring myself, even with the generous medical insurance I was thankfully covered with, I lost most of my savings and am only just now starting from scratch again.

I was exaggerating about the comparative size of my apartment to his laundry, but now as I slowly do a three-hundred and sixty degree turn to take in my surroundings, the contrast seems even more absurd.

Something of my discomfort must show on my face because Ted's expression morphs into concern. That's becoming a pattern with us already, and I can't help but feel that maybe it's a sign that pursuing a relationship with him isn't a good idea after all.

Before he can question me, I blurt, "I'm sorry. Your home is gorgeous. It's just…" I exhale. "Intimidating?"

His handsome face flickers with disappointment and something that looks almost like regret before he schools it into something more sheepish and lighthearted. He scratches the back of his neck and gestures wildly around us. "It needed a lot of work when I bought it, and I did much of that myself. It was a project. I like to keep myself busy."

The last sentence has weight behind it that I can't interpret, but I look around again, trying to gauge just what kind of manual labor he's put into it. As much as I don't try to stereotype, I highly doubt he made any structural changes himself. Or electrical or plumbing. Unless he counts hiring people to do it for him as doing it himself? But he's not like that. Or, at least, he hasn't come off that way in the week I've known him.

As if reading my mind, Ted starts pointing at the walls, "I tore off the old, peeling wallpaper and painted it all myself." He pauses, then rolls his eyes with a playful air. "Alright, sometimes the guys came over to help. Anyway," he points to the floors, "some moron had tiled over the hardwood, so pulling them up, then sanding, staining, lacquering and polishing the floors happened, too. Then there was a lot of minor stuff, just little repairs here and there, and I got contractors in to redo the kitchen, laundry and bathrooms, and the re-carpeting. It took almost a year to get it looking this way."

"Wow," this time when I say the word, it's with more awe than abject horror. "That's…intense."

"Like I said, I like to keep busy."

I want to probe into that, but there's a guardedness to him that prevents me from doing so. I figure we all have our hang-ups and baggage, and it's probably not the sort of thing to be delving into on a first date. Or would this be our second, if you count the wedding?

"So, was the intention to live here long, or are you planning on flipping it?"

Ted rubs his clean-shaven jaw with a large open palm. "Originally, I was going to flip it. It's too big a house for just me. But," he looks around again, his eyes going distant, as if he's reliving the memories of all his hard work, perhaps even memories of horsing around with that tight-knit group of friends of his as they helped, "I think I've gotten attached."

Now I feel a little bit guilty for reacting the way I did. It's obvious that he's put love, sweat and tears into this place, now that I hear him talk about it. To judge it or to judge *him* just because of its size and aesthetics was probably a dick move on my part. I don't think he'd judge me based on my crappy little apartment, after all.

"It is a beautiful home, Ted," I tell him softly, a little bit of my regret slipping into my tone. "I just wasn't expecting it. You seem so down to earth for a lawyer."

A bark of laughter escapes him. "For a lawyer, huh?" He arches an eyebrow at me, then wraps his arms around my waist, pulling me closer to him so we're practically chest to chest with only a few inches of space between us. "Was the addendum necessary?"

"Absolutely," I grin, unrepentant. I don't bother explaining my reasoning. It's much more fun to tease him.

Those amber-brown eyes of his glint down at me and he shakes his head with an almost rueful, yet entirely playful little smirk tugging at his lips. "You're going to be a handful, aren't you?"

I bat my lashes with exaggerated innocence. "Who, me?"

He practically growls a groan, his gaze dropping to my lips.

My heart rate picks up, as if I'm only now noticing our physical proximity or the heat of his arms around my lower back. We've been flirting for a week now and I really want him to lower his head those couple of inches, to act on the fire burning between us. Unconsciously, my tongue darts out to wet my lips.

"Fuck, Zephyr, I'm trying to be a gentleman here," Ted complains, but he doesn't let me go or step back. If anything, his hold tightens, drawing me even closer against him.

"Gentlemen don't say *fuck*, Mister Masters."

My taunt does the trick. He chuckles, shakes his head, and then finally dips down to connect our mouths. But he's restrained, the kiss sweet and chaste, his lips warm and firm against mine. I practically melt into him anyway, parting my lips against his, inviting him to deepen the kiss. He takes the invitation, and our tongues meet and twine together slowly.

We explore each other, cataloging the best angles of our heads and movements of our mouths, setting a rhythm that has me rocking my hips into him without thought, my hands at his hips, fisting into the tight denim of his likely far-too-expensive jeans.

"Oh, tiny dancer, what am I going to do with you?" He murmurs fondly when we part for air. He drops his head lower, nuzzling at the crook of my neck before peppering little kisses up the column of my throat and to the ticklish spot just beneath my ear. I squirm and I feel his resulting laugh rumble through his chest, still pressed against mine. "You're a bad influence, little one."

I want to argue or tease back, but my brain is a puddle of goo right now. I can't recall ever feeling quite so easily attracted to someone before. I've been with handsome men before, but this is the first guy to make my heart stutter and my thoughts disappear. It's not that he's a Daddy, either. I've been with a few Daddies in my time, too. There's just something about Ted and about our connection that fries my internal systems.

Finally, after a moment or two too long to be considered normal, my brain re-engages.

"Do I get the rest of the tour?" I ask breathily, walking my fingers up the center of his short sleeved, button-down shirt. "Someone said something about a playroom?" He's still carrying my bag over his shoulder, and I tap the strap. "We can drop this off in there and then you can follow through on your promise to wine and dine me."

"You know," Ted snickers and sneaks another quick peck to my lips before he rests his forehead against mine, "for someone who said they were looking for a Daddy to take care of them, you're unexpectedly bossy."

"I'm not bossy, I just know what I want."

He pulls back and arches an eyebrow. "You're definitely a princess." Before I can defend myself against the perceived slight against my nature, his face breaks into a breathtakingly gorgeous smile. "I think I'm going to have fun with that."

* * *

The playroom, despite Ted's assurance that the room is a 'standard' sized bedroom, is at least one and a half times the size of the bedroom in my apartment. It's stunning. He has a twin sized bed tucked into the far-left corner from the door, and a white dresser on the wall parallel to it. The walls are painted with a fairy-tale mural, running around the entire room. It's a lush forest full of mythical creatures and characters poking their heads out between trees while dragons and butterflies and unicorns fly through the skyscape above the green treetops. The carpet in here is also a dark, mossy green color, completely different to the white throughout the rest of the house.

A long, low-lying set of shelves, also painted white, runs along the expanse of wall from the walk-in robe to the end of the bed. It is home to a collection of plush toys, a train set, building blocks and one hell of a dollhouse.

I cross the soft carpet to run my finger cautiously over the beautiful item. It's a four story mansion with working lights and opening doors, and I have the urge to play with it immediately.

"You like it?" Ted's gentle question startles me from my inspection of the stunning construction (so much more than a toy), and I turn to face him. He's leaning against the door of the walk-in wardrobe casually, but there's a flicker of something a bit more intense in his eyes.

Taking another glance around the room, predominantly filled with toys and items more suited to 'boyish' play (not that I truly believe that toys are necessarily geared to one gender over another), it clicks, and I feel my jaw drop.

"Please tell me," I swallow roughly, looking back down at the dollhouse, "that you had this exquisite, probably insanely expensive dollhouse *before* I told you about my preference for femme play."

"I had that exquisite, not *that* insanely expensive dollhouse before you told me about your preference for femme play," he semi-repeats dutifully.

I narrow my eyes. "You didn't really, did you?"

The material of his shirt strains across his chest as he raises his arms in surrender. "Does it really make a difference?"

"Jesus, Ted." I take a step back from the collection of toys and shake my head. "We haven't even tried a scene together yet."

"Maybe I just wanted it for my collection. Ash visits. He likes to play teddy bear tea parties. *Maybe* I thought he'd also like the dollhouse."

Well. Damn. He's got me there.

Typical weaselly lawyer. Even though the words are negative, I can't help the fondness I feel when I think them. *This man is definitely going to keep me sharp.*

With twitching lips, I concede defeat. "Alright, that's a fair argument." I look back at the dollhouse, once again overcome by the need to carefully pull it down from the shelf and open it up. It's one of those big, old-school designs with the two halves that open like a book, straight down the middle. "It really is beautiful."

"I'm glad you like it." His tone is all soft and gentle again, and my need changes from wanting to play with the grand 'toy' to wanting his lips on mine once more.

Giving myself a little shake, I look around the playroom one last time and ask to continue the tour. Ted drops my bag by the door as we walk out, and he shows me the rest of the house.

His master suite is like something out of a grand hotel. It's at least three times the size of the playroom, with an enormous bed in the middle of the wall facing the large windows overlooking the city view. Dusk is settling, the sky outside lighting up in orange, peach and pink hues as the sun slowly sets, and twinkling lights begin to speckle the cityscape in the distance. I can imagine sitting on that bed and watching the view for hours, day or night, like a fair maiden in a castle.

Like the rest of the house, the carpets are white. The walls here are more a light gray color, though, and the furniture darker and more masculine. The comforter on the bed is a darker shade of gray, matching the two armchairs nestled in the corner beneath a wrought-iron floor lamp that looks more like art than a functional item. But it's the master bathroom that takes my breath away.

The space is unsurprisingly huge, and tiled from floor to ceiling in large, dark granite tiles with gold flecks, sparkling in the sunlight streaming in from the large window overhanging a massive spa bathtub, built in and surrounded by the same granite as the walls and floor. The tub itself is clearly designed to fit two people comfortably, as is the walk-in shower on the opposite wall, designed as it is with two rainfall shower-heads and a bench seat built into the wall. A long, double vanity stretches in the space between the two decadent wash spaces, and the toilet is positioned on the remaining wall.

With all the dark tile, you would expect it to feel dated or oppressive, but it's somehow still airy and welcoming. It's certainly beyond luxury.

"Fuck me," I mutter, taking it all in, once again feeling out of my depth.

"Okay, I'll admit that I might have gone overboard here," Ted acknowledges, rubbing the back of his neck with a sheepish smile at my reaction. "But I just wanted to spoil myself, I guess. It's not like I have anything else to do with my money." There's that edge again. A hint of melancholy. Maybe regret? He shakes it off and gestures back towards the direction we came from. "The other two bathrooms and the powder room downstairs are all pretty normal in comparison. But this," he waves his arm around, "this was for me."

I finally realize that I have absolutely no right to judge him for spending the money he's worked hard for on the lifestyle he wants to live. He's earned the right to live in luxury if he so chooses. And, from all of our interactions so far, he hasn't seemed at all arrogant or dismissive of those of us (read: me) whose living situations and incomes don't exactly compare. Hell, his social circle, or at least the people I met at Ash's wedding, all seem to be in a similar socio-economic bracket to me, too.

I feel guilty that my reaction to his home has put some sort of divide between us and I make it my aim to fix that immediately. Turning sultry, I saunter over to the tub and lean against its granite frame. "Do you like to soak in this big, beautiful bath, Mister Masters?" Running my finger over the gleaming chrome faucet when he nods, I muse with faux innocence, "With or without bubbles?"

His lips curl upwards and he stalks forward, crowding me with his tall, toned frame. "I am partial to a good bubble bath," he tells me in a low, sexy drawl. "But, I'll admit, it can get a bit lonely in this big tub sometimes."

"Hmm," I make a show of thinking about how I could possibly help him with that dilemma. "Maybe, if you're lucky, we can think of a way to fix that one day."

"You're a real tease, tiny dancer," he groans, but his eyes are glinting with mirth and desire. "And, if you become mine, I will punish you for that."

A shiver of anticipation runs down my spine. *Yes, Daddy.* The words are on the tip of my tongue, but I bite them back. I'm surprised by how readily the title comes to me, but I shouldn't be. We've got real chemistry and our banter has been beyond enjoyable. Not to mention the kiss we shared in the foyer.

"Someone promised me dinner first." My own voice has gone husky, my gaze glued to his lips, wanting another taste but unwilling to make the first move. He's the Daddy here. He needs to take charge. We both know I'll stop him if I'm uncomfortable, and I trust him to respect the boundaries I set.

"Mmm," he agrees, but he closes the space between us and kisses me again, his tongue sweeping against mine, moving his mouth with a hunger that has nothing to do with dinner. It's a kiss full of longing and need and promises full of more to come, and I'm just as lost to it as I was to our first kiss.

As much as I should probably take things slowly with this man, I can feel my resistance slipping, and I'm powerless to stop it.

Chapter Five – Ted

Zephyr's presence does things to me that I just can't explain. I usually pride myself on my self-control. On my ability to remain stoic and firm and guarded when necessary. But with Zephyr I feel like the babbling, fumbling, insecure teenager I was thirty years ago. It's both exhilarating and nauseating.

Especially when I do that math. When I was younger, I was closer in age to the boys that are my 'type'. But, as I've aged, my type hasn't really changed.

There have been times I wished that my tastes were more varied. Turning down Matt's advances when we first met was difficult because he was, and still is, a very sweet man. However, I couldn't force myself to be interested, no matter how compatible our kinks are. It wouldn't have been fair on either one of us, and it would inevitably have ended poorly. Instead, we were able to build a friendship, and he found a Daddy much better suited to him.

And still my tastes haven't changed. I understand that

committing to a relationship means watching your partner age alongside you, but it doesn't mean that I'm not still drawn to men of a certain build or appearance. I just can't help it.

And now? There are fourteen years between Zephyr and me. It does make me a little uncomfortable.

At least it's not seventeen years. That's my magic number. A line I can't cross.

My initial draw to the BDSM Daddy/Little lifestyle is not something I like to dwell on often. My motivations were unhealthy, to say the least. I was young: barely twenty and an absolute mess, and I was looking to prove that I had paternal skills. Looking to prove that I had the ability to nurture and protect and care for a Little. But I was doing it for *all* the wrong reasons. Reasons that make me feel sick to admit now.

That's not what I want to dwell on now.

Besides, through therapy, I eventually worked through all the old pain and regrets and came to love being a Daddy and being involved in the lifestyle in a healthier way. I still want to nurture and care for my boys, but not because I feel like I have anything to prove. It's for my enjoyment as much as it is for the Littles. I like to be someone's rock. I like to provide for them and make sure they're looked after and can live their lives joyfully. If anyone has the means, it's me. And it makes me feel good to make them feel good.

But it's not often that I'm taken off balance with a boy. Over the years, I've found that the interactions I have with most Littles are all similar. There are the shy ones, the bratty ones, the sweet ones, the clingy ones…but Zephyr? He's unlike most boys I've spent time with in the last few years. He's an enigma to me.

He's certainly one of the most brazen Littles I've had the

pleasure to meet. Oozing with confidence and sensuality, he's feisty and challenging and funny. If I had to label him, I'd say he's more Middle than Little, but there are moments where the bravado melts away and I catch glimpses of his more innocent side.

In the week we've spent exchanging texts and talking on the phone, I've picked up clues which lead me to believe that, as confident as he is as a Little, Zephyr hasn't had as much experience with an ongoing relationship with a Daddy. His life until recently hasn't allowed for it, so what experience he has had has been scene play at best.

I've made it clear that I'm more interested in an exclusive, long-term relationship. I know that's new to him. I don't want to rush him but, at the same time, all I want to do is wrap him in my arms and refuse to let him go. It's not normal for me to feel this way. I don't usually get so invested so soon.

It could be that I'm just rattled by other things going on in my life. It's coming up on thirty years since…

No. Nope. Not going there.

Instead, I lose myself in the kiss I've just initiated. Our second. I wanted to respect his wishes to take things slowly, but his flirting threw all my restraint right out the window.

He tastes sweet against my tongue, not a surprise given that he's confessed he has an epic sweet tooth. His body is firm, lean, and pliable under my hands as I slowly explore the plains of his hips and back and shoulders. At thirty-three, he's in the prime of his life, his body perfect for his career in dance. He's already teased me over the phone, taunting me about how *bendy* he is, and I want so badly to put the naughty thoughts that information inspired to the test.

We're flush against each other and my cock twitches when

he mewls against my lips. Unconsciously, I grind against his abdomen, seeking friction.

"Mister Masters," he separates our mouths to breathe with exaggerated scandal, his breath ghosting over my lips as if daring me to capture his mouth all over again, "dinner first, remember?"

I want nothing more than to turn him around, bend him over the tub and plunge inside him, but the playful lilt of his voice reminds me that tonight is a test. A test for our compatibility and chemistry (which I'm certain we've passed with flying colors, if I do say so myself). But also a test of whether there is a possibility for something deeper and more real to develop between us. Making everything about sex won't help prove that we can hold more than simple conversations.

Still, I nip at his lips again before I withdraw and adjust my aching cock, much to his amusement. "I did promise dinner, yes."

His gaze lingers on the bulge in my jeans, and he makes a show of adjusting himself as well, which I shouldn't find as much of a relief as I do. I suppose it's good to know that he's just as affected as I am, that's all.

Leading him back downstairs to the kitchen, he slides onto one of the tall bar stools in front of the long kitchen counter and watches as I pull out my pre-prepared veggies and ingredients for the simple stir-fry I'm cooking tonight.

"Were you a boy scout as a kid?" he asks playfully, gesturing to the cling-film covered bowls I've set out in order next to the stove.

"Actually, I was," I laugh. "My parents were…" I search for the right word and settle on, "traditional, I guess."

They were also devout Catholics who did everything they

could to try and steer their obviously gay son towards 'manly' activities, but I don't mention that. My childhood wasn't miserable, just tense at times. Then, when I left for college with a full-ride scholarship and officially came out of the closet, it became a moot point completely.

Zephyr seems to pick up on some of what I very carefully did not say, because his expression softens and he makes a movement as though he's trying to reach for me across the bench top. His hands fall back into his lap, and he rallies. "Well, mine were anything but. They put me in dance classes of all sorts and, when it looked like I enjoyed Ballroom the best, they set me on the competition circuit. And, when I wasn't doing that, I was being hauled to different sports try-outs, baking classes, 'Mommy and me' yoga sessions…" He shakes his head, his love for his parents paired with fond exasperation. "They wanted to give me a slice of everything."

They sound like everything my parents were not. But there's likely a generation between them, I'm guessing, so it's hardly astonishing that their values and experiences would be different.

"They sound like wonderful people," I tell him honestly, and start tossing ingredients into the wok I've oiled and heated. The meat and veggies sizzle enticingly. "Mine…well, they meant well. Mostly." I shrug. "It was a different time, and they were older when they had me, too."

I'd been a surprise to them, actually. After years of trying for children, they'd given up. Then, in their mid forties, along I'd come. It was a pity they felt I'd been more disappointing than miraculous in the end.

Once again, I realize that I've brought the mood down and I fight the urge to pinch the bridge of my nose.

What the hell is wrong with me?

"Are they…I mean…have they…no, that's not an appropriate date question. Forget I said anything." Zephyr winces and looks away.

If anything, the gaffe makes me chuckle. "They've both passed, yes." I answer lightly, lifting and dropping my shoulders as though it's no big deal. "We weren't close. We pretty much lost touch after I left home for college and, as callous as it sounds, it was for the best for all of us."

When they didn't even reach out during the worst year of my life, even after I told them what had happened at the time, I wrote them off completely.

"I'm still sorry for your loss, Ted."

"Thank you."

Silence descends between us, broken only by the sounds of meal cooking in front of me. This is not how I want the date to go. I want to prove that we can maintain effortless conversation, not back each other into awkward silences.

"Anyway," I forge on when the strange moment has stretched on a little too long for comfort, "the boy scout thing. I've always been a little, uh, anally retentive."

My turn of phrase has the desired effect and Zephyr snickers. "Have you now?"

"Yeah. I like things neat and tidy. I'm methodical. I don't love surprises."

With a wooden spoon in my hand, I turn to catch the widening of his eyes. "But…you're a Daddy," he argues with confusion. "Aren't Littles the antithesis of neat and tidy? Or am *I* the odd one out?"

"Some activities can get messy, sure," I tilt my head in recognition of his argument, "Finger painting, blocks strewn across the room, toy cars scattered…but that's only momentary. In my house, toys are cleaned up and packed away neatly after play. It's a rule." I pin him with a pointed smirk, waggling the spoon in his direction. "The overarching arrangement of Daddy/Little role play is structured. Most Littles thrive on routine as much as I do. And, as Daddy, I get to set those rules and routines. I get to manage the variables as much as anyone possibly can."

"Ah," he leans across the counter now, propping his pretty face up in his palms with his elbows braced on the marble. There's an almost feline grace in the stretch of his long back. He's breathtaking. "And that's why my *bossiness*, as you so kindly put it, eats at you, huh? Don't like being challenged?"

"On the contrary," I face the stove behind me again, giving the simmering meat, veggies and sauce another stir, gauging that it'll only need another minute or two before I can toss in the noodles and then serve it up, "I'm a lawyer because I love a challenge, too."

"So…what does that mean in terms of us, then?" He's so direct and I love it.

"Well," I toss the noodles in early. Fuck it. It won't make much difference. "I'd say that you speak to both sides of me. The lawyer and the Daddy." Now I turn back and smile at him warmly. "And I like that very much."

It's gratifying to watch his own smile blossom across his features, like he feels similarly to me.

But I remind myself that I promised Ted not to rush him, so I carefully add, "I know the concept of an exclusive, long-term thing is new to you, so I won't push. I want tonight to be about showing you how things could be. But there's no pressure, okay? We'll take this all at your pace."

Zephyr's smile morphs into one of gratitude and he nods. "I appreciate that, Ted."

Then I serve up our meal and we move to the dining table, turning the conversation to lighter, happier topics.

* * *

"That was delicious," Zephyr declares, leaning back in his chair and rubbing his belly in an adorably childish sort of way. I like to think that he's loosening up, allowing his Little side to come out and play.

"I can't take all the credit," I confess, pushing back my chair and collecting our empty bowls. "This was London's recipe. Matt raves about it, and London insisted it was quick and easy to make."

"Well, then, you did a good job of following the recipe, anyway." He smiles lazily up at me, his eyes hooded with post-meal sleepiness. It's insanely adorable. I can't prevent myself from bending to kiss the tip of his ski-dip nose. "Mmm," he says, then tilts his head back and puckers his lips for a proper kiss.

Oh, this boy. This beautiful, perfect boy.

I press my lips to his chastely, savoring the brief connection before straightening up and taking our dishes into the kitchen. I pop them into the dishwasher and then pull the chocolate mousse I'd prepared earlier from the fridge.

Zephyr's eyes widen when I set his bowl in front of him. "You're trying to make me explode," he complains. "I wish I'd known there was dessert before I ate so many noodles."

Grinning, I lift a spoonful to my mouth. "I promise, if you can't finish it, you can take a doggy bag home with you."

He pokes his tongue out at me before diving in, and I love that he's starting to get comfortable enough to be cheeky in this way. It's more innocent than his earlier teasing. More childlike and pure.

The moan he releases when the chocolate hits his tongue, though, is anything but.

My cock takes interest at the sound immediately.

"*Oh*," he stretches the sound out, closing his eyes and sucking the spoon until his cheeks hollow, "Ted. This is incredible."

If I didn't know any better, I'd say he was turning dessert into sex on purpose.

He goes for another spoonful. It gets the same treatment, his pink tongue wrapping around the utensil as he makes inappropriate noises and licks it clean. Then he does it again.

I drop my spoon into my bowl with a clatter and splat.

Zephyr looks up, startled.

I can only imagine what the look on my face must be like. My pulse is racing, my cock straining in my underwear, my body rigid with need for him. With the need to hear him make those sounds in a different setting. With my cock in his mouth. In his ass.

Realization seems to dawn on him and embarrassment settles in over his pretty face. "Oh. Uh. I didn't mean…" he stammers, and I see his cheeks darken with the faintest hint of a blush on his flawless skin.

"Oh, no," I practically purr, using all my reserves to keep my hands to myself, even though I want to cup his face in my hands and kiss him stupid again. "I like that I'm able to get those beautiful sounds out of you, even if it's only my cooking that does it for now."

For now.

For all that I keep reminding myself not to push him, I can't help letting these little hopes of mine slip out. Thankfully, he just smiles bashfully and bites his plump lower lip.

"I told you I had a sweet tooth," he defends himself, drifting back into that sweet playful mood he was in.

"You did. And I couldn't help but indulge it."

It appears I can't help myself at all around him.

"Do you spoil everyone, Ted?" he asks from beneath lowered lashes, bringing another spoonful of his chocolate treat up to his lips. I can't tear my gaze from the spoon, watching as he sucks it in and swallows his treat, this time more conscious of the sounds he was making. Not quite enough to completely prevent his delight, but he no longer sounds like something I'd find on PornHub. "Or is this you wooing me?"

"I want to say it's just an attempt to woo you, but it would be a lie," I admit, content to watch him continue to eat, my own bowl forgotten on the table in front of me. "I enjoy looking after people. Making them happy."

"Then what the hell possessed you to become a lawyer?" His question seems to have bypassed his internal filter, because he looks up at me with wide, surprised eyes. "Shit. I'm sorry. That was rude."

A bark of laughter escapes me. "It was a fair question, though. But," I shoot him a firm stare, "I have a rule about watching your language, tiny dancer. My boy…my *princess*," I correct myself, "won't swear."

Cocking a perfectly manicured eyebrow at me, he smirks. "Am I your princess, Ted? Have we started to play?"

"Not yet," I concede. "But I think, if it's something you would like to do, we should go over the rules. I know we've spoken about limits, and we've got our safe words—"

"Meatloaf," he cuts me off with a laugh, then rolls his eyes at me when I don't follow his train of thought. "You know, 'cos I will 'do anything for love'—"

I groan, seeing exactly where he's taking this. "But you *won't do that*." I finish for him dryly, appalled at the joke. "That's awful."

He giggles madly in the face of my put-upon disgust. The sound is joyful and lights me up from the inside.

I push it a little further, exaggerating my reaction. "You're not actually using Meatloaf as your safe word, right?"

"I should," he continues to giggle and then scrapes at his bowl with his spoon, trying to get the last remnants of his mousse into his mouth. I half expect him to abandon the spoon and try to lick the bowl clean, considering the intent look on his face as he goes about his task. "But, no, I use the traffic light system."

It's what we had discussed on the phone and it's also my go-to. "Good." I'm back to being serious. "So. Rules?"

He pushes his empty bowl away with a mournful glance and then looks at me with bright eyes. "So far, I know about cleaning up after we play with toys and not swearing."

"Good boy," I praise, beaming when he grins back at me. "There's also being honest at all times, following instructions, asking questions if you don't understand something, and telling me if there's something new you'd like to try."

He considers these and bobs his head thoughtfully. "They're all pretty common sense."

"I'm glad you think so," I approve. Then I add, "And, as part of following instructions, there will be consequences for things like talking back and sassing me." I give him a knowing stare. He's definitely the sassing type.

His dark eyes glimmer in amusement, even though he feigns innocence. "Would I do that?"

"I think we both know you will."

It's not even a maybe. He's going to push the limits because he can and, oddly, I am looking forward to it. I've never enjoyed brattier play from my Littles before, but I get the feeling Zephyr knows just how far he can take things before he crosses a line from fun to frustrating.

He runs his tongue along his front teeth. "Hmm, so what sort of consequences are we talking about here?"

I can feel my face twisting into a wicked smirk. "It depends on the severity of the infraction, of course. How many warnings I've given, that sort of thing. But I escalate from writing lines and corner time, to spankings, paddling and orgasm denial. Maybe some light humiliation play if you're okay with it." I shrug. "Sometimes the consequences are for fun and we'll both be aware that it's just a game, but other times they're serious. Obviously, we'll talk things through if it's serious."

"I…" Zephyr pauses, surprise coloring his tone. "I don't think I've ever needed a *serious* punishment. Like, it's always just been playful. Sexy. Fun."

"Well, you also said that you've only ever really done the odd scene with Daddies in clubs, right?" He nods and I continue. "It's different when you're in a full-time Daddy/Little relationship. Sometimes behavior needs actual correction. Take the cussing, for instance. I'd make you write lines and neither one of us would actually enjoy that. But it would be to make a point."

He thinks this over some more, drumming his fingers on the tabletop. "But safe words still apply?"

I reach for his hand and squeeze it in reassurance. "Always, little one. You safe word at *any* time and we stop and talk about it."

"Okay," he exhales, then straightens his shoulders and smiles warmly at me. "So…are we going to play tonight?"

I push my chair back and hold my hand out to him. "There's nothing I'd prefer to do."

Chapter Six – Zephyr

"What should I call you?" I ask Ted as we make our way back upstairs to the playroom. His large hand envelops mine with warmth and I'm struck by how natural it feels to be doing any of this with him.

"What are you comfortable with?" he asks in return.

"Well, I really like the idea of going straight to 'Daddy', but if that's something you'd prefer to wait on, just in case this doesn't work out…" I trail off, saddened by the thought that there's still that possibility.

Ted stops us just outside the playroom, turning me until we're facing each other. He gently lifts my chin with his index finger, looking me in the eye. "Darling, you can call me whatever your heart desires, okay? Whatever feels right. Go with it." He drops a kiss to the tip of my nose. "And, for the record, I suspect that this is going to work out just fine."

God, I hope so.

I'm now painfully aware of the fact that I like him far too much for this to be just a one-night trial thing.

Guiding me inside the room with a hand on the small of my back, Ted starts talking again. "Now, usually I would help you get dressed, but given that tonight is about easing you into everything, I don't—"

"I want the full Daddy experience," I blurt, cutting him off. "We're doing this properly."

I know I've made the right decision when his eyes light up and his smile goes all sweet and doting. "Alright, then." He scoops my bag up from the floor and moves over to the bed, sitting on the side and rummaging through my things. With care, he pulls out the frilly purple gown I packed myself: my favorite of all my dresses. With it, he also gets out the matching panties with the lacy scalloped edges. He fingers the material of the dress lovingly. "I bet this looks absolutely gorgeous on you."

I feel my own smile turn shy and I shrug. "It's…it's been a long time since I wore any of my femme stuff," I confess quietly. "Like…before my injury."

His eyes snap up to meet mine, understanding painted on his face. "Well, that's going to make tonight even more special, then, isn't it?"

I hope so, I think again. I'm still worried that the magic is gone. That I won't feel the way I used to. That everything working up to this point will have been for naught. That I'm not the person I thought I was. That my injury took even this away from me.

"Alright, tiny dancer," Ted's voice is low and lulling, "you're thinking too hard. Time to let go and relax."

He reaches for my hands and tugs me forward so he can help me undress. I close my eyes, breathe deeply, and reach for my littler side. It's been so long since I've really gone for it that I almost feel silly. But Ted continues to murmur encouragements and soft praise, carefully pulling my shirt over my head and my jeans and underwear down my legs. By the time I'm completely naked, I'm strangely relaxed.

Ted gently taps my left thigh, silently helping me step into one leg hole of my pretty panties, then the other. He pulls them up, runs his fingers under the elastic bands until they're sitting properly, then holds up my dress. "Arms up, darling."

I comply and he steps into my space again, carefully easing the mess of satin and tulle over my head. My hands slip through the delicate cap sleeves and he helps ease the whole thing down over my body. Then he turns me and pulls the zip up at the back. When I turn back around to face him, the material of the skirt swooshing over the middle of my thighs just as I remembered it would, he steps back to get a good look at me.

"Perfect," he declares.

"Thank you," I curtsy, leaving off the title we've discussed using. I'm not quite little enough yet, still getting used to being back in my old gown. But I'm close to it, and he's not pushing me. That settles me a little bit further.

He laughs, and the sound is rich and warm and full of affection. Then he reaches for my hand, asking, "Should we break in the dollhouse, tiny dancer?"

I don't need to be asked twice. I nod excitedly and together we walk the couple of steps over to the shelves and lift the large item up, carrying it to the middle of the room. We place it on the floor carefully, and I undo the latch that keeps the two halves together. Ted helps me open the house up wide.

The inside is just as beautiful as I imagined it would be. It's decorated in creamy colored tones, with white accents and lace embellishments. There are exquisite bedroom scenes, a ballroom, a library, decadent sitting rooms, bathrooms and a large kitchen.

Shaking me from my visual exploration, Ted sets a large box in front of me. I hadn't even noticed him wandering away to get it. "Now, this is just a start," he says, gesturing for me to lift the lid.

When I comply, I find gorgeous pieces of miniature furniture, all in matching stained dark timber. There are also a couple of small dolls for me to play with as well, and I find that they are just the right size to fit on the furniture.

"They're so pretty," I tell him in awe, carefully lifting each piece out to inspect them individually. I start placing them in appropriate rooms inside the dollhouse as I do. Even though the box is large, I can see what he meant by this collection being 'just a start', because it barely fills a third of the house. But that doesn't bother me at all. I can use my imagination to fill in the rest.

I'm a little surprised when he sits beside me and picks up one of the dolls, joining me in my play. Together, we take our toys on a journey through the home. They dine in the large, formal dining room and we pretend that we're part of their very fancy dinner party, and then the dolls dance in the ballroom. Finally, they bathe in the large bathtub before we send them to bed.

As the dolls sleep, I muse on how enjoyable this has been. It's a new experience for me to spend time with a Daddy who engages in the story with me rather than sitting back to watch me entertain myself. And it didn't seem to be a half-assed attempt on his part, either. He made conversation with the dolls, he offered ideas to extend their activities within their home, and he even spoke with silly, high-pitched character voices, making me giggle raucously. It was like he actually enjoyed playing with me, and *that* thought makes my heart race.

"Can we play something different?" I ask, deciding that the dolls probably need to rest after such an eventful day. Then I remember the rules. "We can pack this up first."

"Good boy," he praises, and the words light me up from the inside. I start to carefully pack away the furniture and the dolls, and he helps me to make the task go faster. Then we put the dollhouse back up on the shelf, once again closed and latched, before he turns to me and asks, "What would you like to play next?"

I've dropped far enough into Little space that I'm honestly excited at the prospect of anything. My eyes land on the tub of blocks on the bottom shelf and I know exactly what I want to do. "Can we build a castle?"

Ted smiles widely and nods, helping me pull the plastic tub out, carrying it to where we'd been playing with the dollhouse. He upends the entire thing and I gasp at the mess it makes, delighting in the familiar click-clack racket of the little wooden pieces tumbling about, muted by the carpet as they fall.

"Are we building a tall castle?" he asks, watching me with obvious amusement as I start to meticulously sort the pieces into colored piles.

"Yep." I pop the 'p'. "Super tall."

"Here," he slides the lid of the tub down between us and then settles himself into a cross-legged position. "It'll be sturdier than trying to build on the carpet."

"Clever Daddy." I tell him, barely aware that I've gotten comfortable enough to let the word slip out. It's only the hastily smothered sharp inhalation from across the small, carpeted space that has me realizing what I've done.

I look up from my stash of brightly colored blocks to catch a sweet smile on his face, but he doesn't bring it up. He just points down at the large, rectangular piece of firm plastic that separates us and asks, "So, where do we start?"

* * *

"Daddy, *stop*," I giggle, squirming away from fingers determined to tickle me into submission, "that's cheating!"

I have no idea how long we've been playing for at this stage. Tonight has well and truly surpassed how I'd hoped the evening might go. I managed to sink so deeply into Little space that, once I started coming back out, I was surprised that it had happened so easily.

Right now, Ted is easing me back into my adult head space with an old-fashioned game of 'Go Fish', only we've moved onto the twin bed in the playroom because Ted's declared his back wasn't made for sitting on the floor for extended periods of time. As with all the other games we've played, he seems just as engaged and genuinely into playing this with me as I've felt all night.

Except he started blatantly cheating and, when I lunged for his cards, it earned me a tickle attack.

"Excuse me, but who tried to take all my cards away?" he argues back, all lawyerly and devastatingly handsome with those twinkling eyes and smug smile of his.

"Because I caught you picking cards out of the pile when you thought I wasn't looking."

Ted is unrepentant. "Daddy's rules say I can."

"Daddy's full of...uh..." I manage to censor myself just in time, smiling sheepishly when one of his eyebrows wings upwards. "Poop?"

Snorting, Ted waggles his index finger at me. "You can get away with that this one time, princess."

That works for me. I smile as innocently as possible and bat my lashes. "Yes, Daddy." I surprise even myself with the sexual undertone in my voice.

I'm back out of Little space and the air between us suddenly feels charged.

"Should we pack the cards away?" Ted asks me after a short span of silence.

I nod.

He gathers them up silently, slipping them into the pack with practiced ease. He tosses the pack onto the little bedside table and then extends his arms. "Come cuddle and talk?"

I take in the vision of him, his shoulders loose and his back propped up with a pillow against the wall behind him. There's still no expectation in his expression or in the way he holds himself. He seems content and relaxed, and maybe a little hopeful, but I can tell that his request doesn't have any underlying agenda. He really does just want to cuddle and talk.

I crawl over the comforter and into his embrace and we maneuver until we're both comfortable, with his chest pressed against my back and his arms, toned and strong, casually draped over my shoulders and coming to rest over my abdomen, crossed lightly at his wrists.

"So, tiny dancer," he says quietly, his voice a low purr, "have you had fun tonight?"

My lips lift upwards at the memories we've just made. "I have." I sigh happily and snuggle in closer, enjoying the feeling of being held. "I didn't think it would be so easy."

I feel him press a kiss to the top of my head. "I'm glad that it was."

I hesitate only briefly before I tell him, "I think a lot of that is because you made it easy for me."

"I didn't do anything special, Zephyr."

"Bull—" I stop myself short as he clears his throat. "I mean, uh, bologna."

Ted snorts.

Smiling to myself, I try to organize my thoughts. Exploring our dynamic really did feel more natural with Ted than it has with any of the Daddies I've done scenes with before. I've never had a bad experience, but I've also never felt so *right* with another Daddy, either…not that my life to this point has really allowed me many opportunities to give it a red-hot go, to be fair.

"I'm serious, though." I eventually say, glad that Ted has allowed me a chance to try and process my thoughts properly. "I've never really had a Daddy get so into the games before. Like, sure, I've done tea parties where Daddies have joined me, but…you make it feel like you're actually enjoying what we're doing, not just the fact that we're role playing as Daddy and boy." I lean my head back on his shoulder so I can awkwardly look at his face. "Does that make sense? Like, I know they enjoyed playing the role of Daddy, but you seemed to really appreciate *what* we were doing. Ugh. I don't think this is coming out right."

A chuckle rumbles up through his chest, vibrating against my back. He kisses my forehead. "I think I'm following you. And I did have fun playing along." He pauses. "I'm sure those other Daddies do, too, in their own way. But we all get something different out of this stuff, you know?"

"Hmm," I consider, though I'm not sure I completely agree

with him. "Well, is this the sort of thing you can see yourself doing more often? I know you're more used to…" I fumble over my words, gesturing vaguely with my hands, "I guess what is seen as stereotypically 'boyish' play."

I'm relieved that he doesn't just answer automatically. I want to know that he's really considering his needs, too.

After a comfortable stretch of silence, Ted finally says, "You know what? I can. Ultimately, for me, being a Daddy…or," he seems to correct himself, "in this case, being *your* Daddy is about the same thing, regardless of the scenes themselves." He shuffles our position so I lean more to the side and he can look me in the eye. "I want to look after you, Zephyr. I want to play with you, take care of the things that cause you stress, make sure you're eating well. I want to be your safe space and your rock: there for anything you need when you need me. Whether you're playing with teacups or cars makes no difference. I just want to spend time with you."

"Um, wow." I was not expecting that barrage of heartfelt information, but it gives me all the warm fuzzy feelings.

In hindsight, I can't say I'm all that surprised. Ted's a lawyer. It makes sense that he's a bit wordy. Especially when he specializes in contract law. Gotta cross all the 't's and dot all the 'i's or whatever.

I nuzzle my face into his shoulder and respond the only way I can. "I want to spend time with you, too."

Chapter Seven – Ted

Zephyr's reply to my overthought ramblings is a relief. I can't help the silly smile that stretches my face. "You do?"

"Uh huh." He beams back. Then his expression turns exaggeratedly coquettish and he's looking up at me from beneath his long, dark eyelashes in a way that has my cock taking interest immediately. "So…" he draws the word out, sounding far too sultry for me to miss his intention, "maybe we should do something you like now, huh?"

Still, I play dumb, wanting to see where he's going with this. "Oh? What do you suggest?"

"Well, you *did* say you like to take baths, didn't you?"

Oh, God yes.

With the way we're snuggled together in a position meant to be completely innocent when I suggested that we cuddle and chat, there's no way he doesn't feel me react to the images he's just put in my head. Especially not when he moves to get more comfortable again, moving his head back to my shoulder with the length of his body practically plastered against me again. My voice is low and husky when I admit, "I did."

His perfect, plump lips draw into a self-satisfied smirk. "Do you want to share a bath in that ridiculously oversized tub of yours, Ted?"

There's no sign of his Little side now, even if he is still dressed in his little princess gown. Beneath the cute veneer is a siren who knows exactly what he's doing. He's insanely sexy, all youthful, lithe and confident, and it's beginning to dawn on me that our dynamic is going to be more complex than I'd first assumed, but in all the best ways.

My previous relationships have always followed a more predictable Daddy/Little pattern where I'm the dominant partner and primary caretaker. But there's nothing predictable about Zephyr. Right now, I'm getting the distinct impression that I might be Daddy, but he's going to rule the roost. Or he's going to try to.

"I would love that," I answer him, and he brings his hand behind his hip, cupping my *very* interested erection, causing me to suck in a sharp breath.

His answering chuckle is wicked. "Uh huh," he acknowledges, "so I see. Well, feel."

"*Zephyr…*" I lower my voice in warning and he laughs with delight.

"Oh, your Daddy voice is *perfect*." He wiggles his ass, teasing me further. "More of that, please."

Is this a punishable offense? 'Funishable', really. It's too damn good to actually want him to stop. My brain is slowly turning to mush as he continues to grind back on my cock.

"You're being extremely naughty, tiny dancer," I give him the exact reaction he's looking for, leaning down and moving my mouth down to the junction where his elegant neck meets his smooth shoulder. I nip at the skin I find there. "If you keep going, there *will* be consequences."

Rubbing his cheek against mine, I can feel his lips quirking. "What kind of consequences, *Daddy*?"

"Hmm," I hum, pretending to consider my options. My lips travel to the shell of his ear. He shivers as I whisper, "You seem to like teasing. Maybe edging you would be appropriate."

"*Oh…*" Zephyr mewls and rocks his hips.

It's all I can do to keep my hands relaxed over his chest instead of gripping those same hips to encourage even more delicious friction. However, I do allow myself to suck his earlobe for a moment before quietly asking, "You like that idea, kitten?"

"Mmm," he answers, rocking back against me for a few more beats, then gives himself a little shake. "So, uh, bath?"

It takes me a minute to focus and remember how we'd gotten to this point, the sensation of him rubbing against me providing a delicious distraction that I don't mind disappearing into. But then his words float through the lusty fog in my head and I realize that sharing a bath means being naked together. I can't agree fast enough.

"Come on," I give him a playful little push off my lap so we can both scoot off the bed, "let's go before I decide keeping you in this bed with me is just as enjoyable."

He laughs and climbs off, waiting patiently for me to follow. He doesn't disguise the way his heated gaze travels the length of my body, zeroing in on the bulge in my jeans.

But, even though I can see the desire on his face, I'm all about consent and communication, so I soften my gaze. "This isn't too fast for you?"

Shaking his head, he smiles back, a hint of coyness in his

expression. "No. I mean, you've seen me naked already, so I'd really like to even the playing field."

"Well, I can't argue with that logic," I chuckle. "But there's no pressure for this to be anything more than just a bath, okay?"

"I appreciate that. But, trust me, I want you naked. *Now.*"

* * *

The bath water is just the right side of hot when I sink into it behind Zephyr with a pleasured sigh. Even though the tub is large enough to fit us side by side, I'm sitting in the middle with him cradled in the V of my legs, his back pressed against my chest in a mirror image of the way we'd been on the bed earlier. We're immersed in bubbles, but I can feel and picture every inch of his smooth skin where it meets mine.

We took our time undressing as the bath filled, teasing each other with light touches and chaste kisses. This entire evening has been a whirlwind of exploration between us. We've been hot and heavy, innocent as Daddy and boy, flirtatious as equals, and now we're sharing this sedate, relaxed interaction. It's almost like it has been a taster event: sampling the treasures that a relationship together can provide.

"What are you thinking, tiny dancer?" I ask into the comfortable silence after a few minutes spent just enjoying the sensation of having his slippery, wet form on mine. "Are we going to give this thing between us a real shot?"

You would think that the fact that we've progressed this far so quickly would assure me that tonight has been a success, but I like having things confirmed definitively. And, even though he agreed earlier that he wants to spend time with me, I want to talk it through properly. I want to be sure we're on the same page. That 'spending time together' as a concept for him is the same as it is for me: an exclusive relationship, with me as his Daddy full-time, whether he's big or little.

"I've wanted to since you called and asked me out," he answers on a sigh, practically melting into my chest. Beneath the water, I can feel his hand running up and down my thigh soothingly. "Tonight has been everything I'd hoped it would be and more."

I can feel my heart leaping for joy. "Me too," I admit, beaming a smile before bending to kiss the top of his head. "So… dating?" It's an inadequate word for everything I want to do and everything I want to be for him. "Exclusively?"

Zephyr moves, twisting his body around until his long legs are wrapped around my waist and our cocks are brushing against each other beneath the bubbles. Water sloshes around us, slapping at the sides of the tub, but I'm focused on his face.

His expression is a sweet mixture of hopeful and bashful. "I'd like that."

"Good." The single word is all I can manage before I crash our lips together.

This kiss is much like our earlier ones, hot and demanding. Our tongues play together as though fighting for dominance. My hands scrabble for purchase on his slippery wet skin, sliding over sinewy muscle and the toning of years of dancing and aerobics. His hands are trapped between us, fingers splayed over my chest, tangling in my coarse chest hair, plastered as it is to my skin.

The sounds of the water lapping and gently splashing as our bodies rock together battle with our breathy moans and pants. When I keep one hand supporting Zephyr across his back and reach between us with the other to stroke both our dicks together, Zephyr keens into our kiss.

"*More*," he begs, bouncing in earnest now.

Water flows over the sides of the tub, but I couldn't care less. I tighten my grip and pump us harder, chasing bliss for both of us.

"Fuck, kitten," I practically growl when he jerks away from our kiss to bite at my earlobe and breathe heavily with his building release.

"*Ted*," he whines plaintively. "Ted, I need to come. Please, Ted. *Please*."

I vaguely recall my threat to edge him, but denying him his orgasm right now also means denying mine, and I already feel like I've been teetering close to the precipice for hours.

"I've got you," I tell him, my own voice tight and gravelly with desperation. "Come for me, darling. Come over my cock."

He throws his head back, exposing the elegant column of his neck, droplets of water and sweat making him shimmer in the low lighting of the bathroom. "Oh, *oh*," he cries, his face contorting into the perfect moue of mixed rapture and torture. His hips are practically rocketing into my fist now, his movements seeming to have lost their rhythm. "Shit, shit, shit…I'm…oh, *fuck*." He draws the last word into a long, low moan and I feel his cock swell and spurt ropes of cum into the water between us.

Watching and feeling him go over the edge pushes my orgasm over, too, and I mutter something unintelligible as my release joins his. I continue to lazily pump my fist over us until he squirms and complains that it's too much.

The comedown is slow, filled with lazy kissing and nuzzling as the water around us grows tepid. Then I coerce him out of the tub and into the shower for a quick rinse off. Wrapped in big, fluffy bathrobes once I've dried us both, we move into the bedroom and flop down on top of the covers, both boneless and ridiculously happy.

Before I can ask him if he'd be comfortable staying the night, Zephyr snuggles into me and cheekily asks, "Are you cooking me breakfast in the morning?"

At this rate, I can see me offering to cook for him every morning if it means more moments like this.

Chapter Eight – Zephyr

When I wake up the next day, it takes a minute for the previous night's events to catch up with me. I'm ensconced in warmth, Ted's strong arms wrapped around me like a blanket, the heat of his skin on mine a bigger comfort than I could have imagined it would be. His morning wood is like a burning rod against the base of my spine and it's all I can do to not grind my ass back into him while he's still sleeping.

One of the things I learned about Ted during the week spent texting and talking on the phone is that he's not a morning person. He likes to sleep-in on weekends and, listening to the slow, even breathing behind me, I know that today is no exception.

I don't mind. As I might have expected, his bed is sinfully comfortable. The view through the large windows is just as breathtaking in the early morning sunlight as it is at dusk and at night. I'm content to lie here, snug in Ted's embrace, and just enjoy the peace and tranquility while my thoughts drift.

Going back to last night, I think about just how well the 'test' evening went. It felt more like an established relationship than a first date, and I wonder how much of that can be put down to the week spent getting to know each other and how much can be put down to genuine chemistry. Either way, it was good. Heck, it was better than good to be myself and let go with Ted.

It was also a relief that I was able to sink into my Little head space and femme play far more easily than I thought I would. It had felt like stepping back into my skin, comfortable and homey. I hadn't had to force it, nor did I feel silly or strange. If anything, I felt whole again for the first time in a long time.

As much as Ted tried to downplay his role in that, I know that his complete acceptance and enthusiasm did more for me than I could have achieved in role playing on my own or at a club. Was that why I'd pushed the issue when it came to the bath? I hadn't felt obligated or anything. But I had really wanted to show my appreciation, riding the waves of endorphins and connection that a good scene in Little space had created.

I have zero regrets there.

That bath had been perfect. When he'd added the soap for the bubbles, I'd wondered if Ted had wanted to extend the Daddy/Little play, but that hadn't been the case. It had been for ambiance and the modesty that a cover of bubbles provided, not that either of us had really needed it. Still, there's always an added layer of decadence when bubbles are involved in a sexy bath.

And sexy it was.

If I close my eyes, I can recall the feel of our slick cocks sliding together, of Ted's large hand wrapping around us both, stroking us to completion in the hot water.

"Mmm," a low rumble of appreciation travels up Ted's chest

and warm, wet lips find my shoulder and neck. His hand smooths down my side and over my hip, down to my cock which is hard and leaking for him already, courtesy of my trip down memory lane. "I could get used to waking up like this."

He rolls his hips forward languidly, teasing the crack of my ass with the head of his own erection. I push back instinctively. I've never slept naked with a lover before, but now I can't imagine doing anything else.

"*Fuck*, Zeph," he groans and tightens his grip on my dick.

This latest nickname (because Ted seems to be a fount of them) makes me all warm and gooey inside, despite it just being a shortening of my name. It seems more personal than any of the others and said on a whim at that. Passionate and raw.

My gut swirls with need.

"You've got lube and condoms in here somewhere?"

Instead of answering, Ted rolls away from me and I bite back my complaints when I hear the drawer of his bedside table rolling open and the tell-tale sounds of his rummaging around for the requested items.

"Thank Christ," he utters, coming back to me, victorious. "They're in date." When I crane my neck around to look at him, there's mild embarrassment on his face. "It's been a while. I probably should have thought to replace them before now, but…"

"It's been a while for me, too," I reply, too amped up to be amused by his sweet rambling.

He brings our mouths together and I'm too worked up to worry about my morning breath, and he doesn't seem to care either. We kiss languidly and Ted moves me onto my back, the *snick* of the cap from the bottle of lube the only warning I get before warm, wet fingers are probing at my hole.

"Is this okay?" he asks, teasing the rim with gentle, patient movements. "If you want me to stop—"

Consent is clearly a big deal for him. I genuinely appreciate that, but he needs to trust that I will safe word or stop him if I'm at all uncomfortable. But, before I say anything, the fleeting thought *'what kind of relationships has he had before me to inspire this behavior?'* has the words lodging in my throat.

I know I'm not the neediest Little. I'm big more often than not, and I like a modicum of control over my life. I like to push boundaries and tease for pleasure, not really in a bratty way, and I like to take care of my lovers as much as they take care of me. I know that Ted is a natural caretaker and, if last night is any indication, I'm happy to roll with that. It didn't feel like I wasn't his equal at any part of the evening, even if he was Daddy and I was his boy. I was still calling the shots, just in a different way.

His previous relationships might have been more traditional, though. His Littles more submissive, maybe. Sweeter and softer and more likely to need reassurance.

But that's not me.

I'm not made of glass, and I want him to fuck me already.

"It's better than good," I tell him, grinding down onto his fingers to encourage him to pick up the pace. I meet his gaze, hoping that my need is burning into him. "I promise; if it's not, I'll tell you. Just fuck me, Ted. Please."

His eyes widen and then practically roll back in his head. "You're going to be the death of me."

"But what a way to go, right?"

"*Zeph*," he says in a tone that's an interesting mix of fondness and warning.

"*Daddy*," I chime back in the same tone, cutting myself off with a strangled groan when he plunges his thick index finger inside me. "*Yes*," the 's' in the word turns long and sibilant. "Just like that." I arch my hips up to meet his ministrations. "More."

"I knew it," he mutters, pumping his finger in and out maddeningly slowly, "I knew you'd be a bossy bottom." The words are chiding, but he sounds amused and affectionate.

Whining and wriggling, trying to encourage him to pick up the pace and stretch me further, I begin to tease, "If you think this is boss—" my words are cut off as a pleasured gasp is forced from my lips with the skilled movement of his fingers. "*Oh shit*, yes, there, Ted. *Fuck*."

"Such a naughty mouth on you, too," he laughs, but the sound is breathy and strained, belying his own arousal. "What are the rules, tiny dancer?"

"Really?" I ask, knowing I sound bewildered and incredulous. I raise my head to stare at him in disbelief. "The no swearing thing extends to sex?" For me, that's impossible. I shake my head, dropping it back onto my pillow as he crooks his finger and grazes my prostate. "*Fuck*." I breathe. "Yeah...no. That's a no. You can't enforce — oh, *God*, Ted." The second finger distracts me from my rant, stretching and burning beautifully.

"You were saying?" He sounds smug.

I writhe as he scissors and curls his fingers with practiced ease. "We're renegotiating that rule," I manage after a few moments of indulging in the pleasure. In between pants and sighs, I get out the rest of my bargaining chip. "If you ever want to see what else my mouth can do, you'll let me say whatever the hell I want during sex."

He's quiet as he contemplates my words, his fingers still working me open. "That's fair," he eventually acknowledges, then pulls his fingers out. This time I do complain when he moves aside, but the crinkling of a foil wrapper has me hushing up. However, he takes me by surprise when he rolls the condom over *my* cock, saying, "and, as a gesture of good faith, let me show you what mine can do." Then his mouth engulfs me whole.

My brain shuts down. This fun little back-and-forth between us is impossible to maintain when my dick is surrounded by heat and suction. Then Ted's lubed fingers are back inside me and I'm officially lost to the pleasure he's giving me.

I'm a begging, thrashing mess by the time Ted pulls away from my cock and removes the condom. I want to sob at the fact that I'm so close and yet so far from coming, but he shushes me quietly and reaches across to the nightstand for another condom, this one for him. I struggle to my elbows to watch him roll it on over his thick cock, then spread my legs in invitation for him once it's situated.

He dribbles more lube over himself and lines up, his tall, broader form stretching over mine as he finally pushes in. I breathe through the intrusion, his three fingers barely having prepared me for his girth, and Ted gives me a moment to adjust. Then he takes his time, pitching his hips forward and back in tiny, teasing thrusts until he's bottomed out.

"*Ted,*" my breathing hitches, "you feel...*ungh*..." The gradual, deliberate slide of his cock is indescribable. For all our playful talk about edging and orgasm denial, I get the feeling that Ted likes to draw the pleasure out. It feels amazing to have him inside me, filling me up, grazing in all the right ways as he moves with determined strokes.

"Right there with you," he agrees, breathing heavily. "You're like a vise. It's..." he moans as he pushes back in and closes his eyes, "Zeph, fuck, so tight. So perfect."

I reach up and thread my fingers into his thick hair, the flecks of silver among the brown glinting in the sunlight now streaming through the windows. Tugging his head down, I kiss him hungrily, trying to goad his tongue into a faster pace, hoping that it might then transfer to his hips.

Between us, my cock throbs, practically demanding friction. When Ted pushes in closer, his stomach rakes over the sensitive head and precum dribbles from my tip.

"Touch yourself," he demands against my lips. "Stroke in time with my thrusts."

I don't know that I have it in me to properly obey. Once I get my hand around it, I'm more likely to try and jerk myself to coming as fast as possible.

As if knowing exactly where my thoughts have gone, Ted drops his voice even deeper, adopting that dominant Daddy tone that I find so very enticing. "*Zephyr*," he warns, not losing rhythm. "Slowly."

"Yes, Daddy," I agree, only a *tiny* bit of cheek in my voice because I just can't help myself.

Then I snake my hand down between us and, using my own precum to slick the way, start sliding my fist over my neglected dick in the same leisurely pace that Ted is fucking me.

"Oh, kitten, that's so hot," he says, glancing down between our bodies to watch, mesmerized by my actions. "One day I'll get you to jerk off for me. To show me exactly how you like it."

The idea of putting on a show for him is super enticing and shoots through me like an electric shock. "Yes," I cry out, my balls tightening.

"Don't come yet," Ted demands.

Wait...*what?*

Something of my current tumultuous feelings must show

on my face because his resulting chuckle is almost dark and devious. He presses another kiss to my lips, teasing them open with his tongue and slowly taunting me with it.

"We come together," he says when we part again.

"I'm so close…"

"Hold it for me, Zephyr."

Jesus Christ, he wasn't playing when he said he'd edge me, was he?

I whine.

"Zephyr." Ted's tone is all Daddy again. It sends another spark of pure arousal through me. More precum drizzles over my hand and down my shaft, an obscenely copious amount that says I'm riding a fine line right now.

My tenuous control begins to slip with every measured slide of his cock inside me. I grip my dick tighter, trying to physically hold the release back. I can feel my orgasm building, the tension inside me nearly unbearable, a tingle building in my balls.

"*Daddy,*" this time I do sob the word, all trace of defiance or cheekiness gone. "I can't…I'm gonna…"

"Don't come." His order is firm.

I open my eyes, idly wondering when I clenched them shut, to meet his. They're a bright amber in the sunlight, intense with heat and desire. His jaw is also tense, his shoulders shaking as he starts to increase the strength of his thrusts. He's still moving at a languorous pace, but I can see his control weakening.

"I..I…I…"

"*Fuck,*" he growls, pulling out and *slamming* his cock home. I'm pretty sure I see stars.

"Oh! Oh God, Ted…" My eyes shut of their own accord again,

even though I so desperately want to watch him fall apart as he fucks into me with wild abandon. But I'm still trying to hold back, still trying to obey his order, and I'm not sure I can. Not sure I'll hold out.

"Soon, kitten." His words are separated by both heavy exhalations and rough, hard thrusts of his hips. "I'm almost there."

Hearing that confession is what breaks me. "Oh, oh no," the tell-tale tightening of my balls is almost painful now, the electric jolts of pleasure beginning to override the last vestiges of my control. "Oh shit, oh shit, *oh shit.*" The first spurts are a blissful release, shooting over his stomach and chest.

He drops his lips back to mine, kissing me and riding me through my intense orgasm, then moves them to my ear, whispering a litany of praises and 'Good boy's and 'you feel fucking phenomenal's through groans as his hips jerk and he comes hard inside me.

He collapses on top of me, smearing my cum between us, and we laugh and kiss and roll about in the sheets as the adrenaline and endorphins settle. Somewhere in all that, he pulls out and ties off the condom, wrapping it in a tissue from his nightstand for disposal later.

"That was…*whoa.*" I manage, breathing hard, unable to be any more descriptive than that.

"Mmhmm," he agrees, and I can hear the smile in his voice, but I can't see it because my eyes are shut, and my head is pillowed by his shoulder. The moment feels terribly domestic, but also right.

It's still early enough in the morning that I yawn and settle in for a bit of a catnap. "Can we do it again soon?"

"You're insatiable," he laughs.

I'm too tired to tease back and I allow the sound of his chuckles to lull me back into dreamland.

* * *

"You have flour on your nose," Daddy observes, his head cocked to the side and an indulgent smile pulling at his lips.

I brush my hands over the pretty, frilly pink gingham apron he gifted me earlier and then attempt to dust off my nose. The action only earns me more chuckles.

I'm making pancakes. After our early morning activities (and a super enjoyable shower once we woke up later in the morning) I craved the sweet carbs. I then set about begging for them, discovering quickly that Little Zephyr only needs to bat his eyelashes and Daddy will fold like a…like a…towel! (Okay, so metaphors aren't my strong suit when I'm little.)

I was well and truly in my Little headspace when I skipped into the kitchen, and I didn't question why he already had an apron for me hanging on a hook in the butler's pantry, not even when he presented it to me with a flourish and helped me tie it around my waist.

It's probably something I'll think about later when I'm 'big' again, but for now I'm distracted by the sweet late breakfast I'm trying to make with Daddy's help.

"Come here, kitten," Daddy says when my attempts to clean off my face only serve to fuel his amusement more, "let's clean you up."

With a sigh, I push aside the large bowl of batter I've been adding ingredients to and whipping to a smooth, aerated consistency, and I turn bodily to face Daddy.

He's armed with a wet wipe and carefully, but firmly,

smooths it over my nose and cheeks when I tilt my head back for him. I scrunch my nose and squirm when the cold, moist material meets my skin.

"Daddy, stop," I complain with a whine, but he only chuckles more.

"Patience, tiny dancer," he's finished with the left side of my face and moves on to my right, "almost done."

I wriggle and complain until he releases my face, then I go back to my bowl of batter. I whisk it a bit longer and then, when it's the consistency I like, I turn back to Daddy. He's resting his hip against the counter, seemingly content to watch me work.

I hold the bowl out towards him. "Can you help me cook them, Daddy? I don't wanna get burned."

His eyes fill with the same warmth as when he sat on the floor and joined me as I played last night. "We can't have that," he agrees and takes the bowl from me, placing it on the counter beside the stove where a griddle pan is already waiting.

Producing a ladle, Daddy fiddles with the burners to preheat the pan and then melts some butter on its surface.

"Okay, kitten, ladle a pancake out onto the pan," he says, dutifully helping to guide my hand with the scoop of batter into the center of the heated surface. He helps me slowly tip the thick liquid into a circle, then I drop the ladle back into the bowl with a satisfying splat.

Daddy gives my butt a gentle tap in admonishment. "You'll be the one cleaning up the mess you make," he warns.

"Yes, Daddy."

"Good boy."

Those words thrill me more than I can properly express, and I think he knows it.

"Now, you see how the pancake is bubbling?" he directs my attention back to the pan where the slightly wobbly circle of yellow batter has puffed up and is now dotted with bubbles.

"Yeah?"

"Well, now we flip it very carefully." He hands me a spatula.

As with pouring the batter, Daddy holds my hand over the handle of the utensil. He helps me slide it under the cooked side of the pancake and, with a flick of our wrists, flips it over to reveal golden brown deliciousness.

My mouth waters almost immediately and I take in a deep breath, savoring the sweet, buttery scent.

"Can I have it now, Daddy?"

A snort is my only answer for a moment, but then he says, "We have a whole batch to cook first, darling."

I groan with impatience. I want my fluffy, soon-to-be syrupy treat immediately!

"*Zephyr…*" Daddy's tone is one of warning, but I do love it when his voice goes all low and serious like that. Still, I'm not planning on pushing my luck. I really do want to eat the pancakes.

With eyes wide with extra innocence, I bat my lashes and fiddle with one of the many hems of my frilly apron. "I'll be good, Daddy."

And I am.

It's not too long before I'm seated at the table with a stack of fluffy, perfectly cooked pancakes in front of me, a melting pat of butter seeping into the top one. Daddy pours a generous amount of syrup for me, somehow aware that I can't be trusted to do it myself (my sweet tooth would have me upending the whole carafe), and then I'm digging in with gusto.

Daddy eats his own portion with more refinement and

patience, reaching for the wet wipes when he spies the mess of syrup on my cheeks and fingers.

"You're a bit of a menace, aren't you, little one?" he teases when I squeal and squirm away from the wet cloth again.

I giggle.

When I'm bigger, I'll look back on this interaction as the cherry on top of what genuinely feels like a perfect first Daddy/boy interaction. But for now I'm excited to keep exploring this whole new world of domestic scenes with this handsome man I've found.

Chapter Nine – Ted

"Y ou look like the cat who caught the canary, the mouse, *and* the neighbor's gerbil," Charlie observes with a wide grin when we catch up for drinks on Tuesday evening. He's back from his short honeymoon, back into the daily grind of his kink-friendly community center, but married life looks good on him. "Want to share why that might be?"

He's not the first person to have noticed my good mood since the weekend. Louise has been shooting me knowing smirks since the staff meeting yesterday morning, and even my clients have said I've seemed 'chipper'.

"Yeah, well, what can I say?" I ask, unable to stifle the goofy smile stretching my lips. "Things are good right now."

"It's Zephyr, right? Ash's new friend? The one you were flirting with at the wedding?"

I can't deny it, so I don't. "Yeah."

And if I go slightly doe-eyed at just the mention of his name, I'll blame the insane number of orgasms I've had since Saturday night. That boy is an aphrodisiac all on his own, and I think he's melted my brain.

Charlie raises his glass towards me and I clink mine against it. He's grinning even wider now. "It's about time you found someone who makes you happy."

"I'll drink to that." I bring my beer to my lips and take a healthy swig for emphasis.

"Ash will be over the moon, too," he continues. "Having his Uncle Ted bring another friend around for play-dates will make his year."

"Because marrying the man of his dreams hasn't?"

Charlie laughs and shakes his head. "Nah. The wedding was for my family's benefit and we both know it. We would have been happy enough just to elope to the courthouse."

"And when you say your family—"

"I mean my mother, yeah." Charlie huffs out a fond laugh, shaking his head. "I love her, but she's as crazy as ever." Setting down his beer, he sighs. "She's nagging Maze for grand-kids now. Let me tell you, Maisy is *not* happy about it."

I shift uncomfortably on my bar-stool. Talk of children always unsettles me. "I can imagine." I don't offer any more than that. I can't.

Charlie's former career as a cop is still alive and well inside him because he sits up a little straighter, arching an eyebrow at me with unveiled curiosity. He can tell he's struck a nerve of some kind, and I doubt he's going to let it go. Kids as a concept isn't something we've ever discussed. And why would we? We're BDSM Daddies, which is something *very* different.

"Did you ever want kids?" he asks me and my gut sinks.

We've known each other for a long time. I consider lying to him, because to air this dirty laundry now feels like a bad idea. Like opening Pandora's box, I don't know what's going to happen if I do.

When we first met, he was so young and new to The Grove and getting his footing as a Daddy, and our friendship developed almost accidentally as I answered his questions and took him under my wing. Now he's like a younger brother —*a pseudo son, almost, if not for the fact that he's not quite young enough*— and I know that he's probably not going to understand how I could have kept something quite so huge from him.

But I can't lie. Not to Charlie.

Knowing that I'm about to change everything between us, I take a deep breath and stare into the bubbles inside my golden brew, quietly praying for the strength to get through this conversation.

"I…had a son."

All the joy and warmth from the beginning of our conversation seems to evaporate as the silence hangs between us. Was it only a few minutes ago I was buzzing from the admission that I've got a new boyfriend? Now I'm dragging up memories that are better off buried.

"You…*what?*" Charlie's blue eyes are wide and stunned. Then the past tense in my sentence must hit him because the expression crumples into sympathy. "What…Ted, *shit*. When…" He stops asking questions (the same questions everyone stumbles over when they inevitably find out about Aiden) and just stares.

"He would've been thirty this year." I don't know where the fuck that additional information decided to come from, but I immediately regret it, watching Charlie do the mental math.

"You…you were…"

"Seventeen. Seventeen and stupid." I grab for my glass,

taking another huge mouthful to try and just. stop. talking.

It's been a long time. I've been to therapy. I've worked through the trauma and the pain and…okay, so the grief hits me every so often, but I'm not a mess. I'm not. And, as always, when people hear the story and then work out that it wasn't long after his passing that I turned to BDSM as a *Daddy* no less, well…let's just say the judgment doesn't sit well with me.

"Fuck." Charlie sucks down a third of his own glass before he turns baleful eyes on me. "Why didn't you ever say anything?"

I arch an eyebrow at him. "It's not exactly the easiest thing to slip into conversation."

"Alright, yeah, I get that," he rubs his hand over his bearded jaw. "And you've just been dealing with this on your own?" I shrug, trying to ignore the narrowing of his eyes. "*Ted.*"

"That tone doesn't work on me," I try to joke. "Especially because I taught it to you."

"*Ted,*" he repeats.

I sigh. And then the whole story pours out. "It's a cliché, really. Or it starts with one. I was trying so hard to be straight. My parents…" I wave that mess off with a sigh. "I went to a party, got drunk off my ass, thought it would prove something if I slept with a girl—" I had to imagine the quarterback to get it up "—and, naturally, I got her pregnant."

I close my eyes and tilt my head back, the old memories prickling under my skin unpleasantly. Jess's panic. My own. My parents' reactions. *Ugh.*

"I thought my life was over," I make myself continue. "Our parents forced us to be responsible. I manned up, Aiden was born just after Senior year ended. I was almost eighteen."

I know I sound detached, but I can't let myself go back to that time of my life in detail. I can't. I'll break if I do.

Still, a small smile tugs at my lips at the glimpse of memory I allow myself now. Tiny fingers and toes. Eyes like mine. Jess's button nose. The panic ceasing for the briefest moment as I held him for the first time. "He was perfect. And I was fucking terrified, but somehow we made it work. Until college. Then things got hard."

Charlie reaches across the table, gripping my forearm and squeezing it in a show of silent support. I take another mouthful of beer and steel myself for the worst part.

"I had a full-ride scholarship and had to take it. Unfortunately, it took me half-way across the country. Jess's parents wouldn't let her come with me, and I knew I'd never get custody while they were providing a roof over Jess's and Aiden's heads. So I worked my ass off at college, got a part-time job and sent them whatever cash I had, went back home for long weekends and holidays…" Away from my parents, I finally came out of the closet but didn't date. I had too much going on. "Then, one day, I got hauled out of class by a pair of cops."

I close my eyes, unwillingly picturing the moment as vividly as if it had just happened. It's seared into my brain. The sympathy and sadness on the two guys' faces as they guided me into an empty lecture hall and tore my world apart isn't something I can ever erase.

"There'd been a car accident." Despite my greatest attempts to prevent it, my throat still goes tight and tears blur my vision. "Jess and her parents died on impact. But Aiden…"

I try to clear my throat. To this day, sitting in hospitals makes me feel sick and panicky. The sterile scents, the beeping of machines, the wires and tubes, the eerie silences: I shudder at the thought.

When Charlie was shot, it was like I'd gone back in time. The worry of not knowing if the person you're waiting on is going to come out the other side of the trauma… Well, if I hadn't had Ash to look after when we'd been waiting on Charlie to recover, I honestly would have lost my mind. Of course, none of the guys know any of this.

"I got to say goodbye." This last sentence is all I can manage to force out. I refuse to relive the rest. Thankfully, Charlie doesn't push for more.

"*Jesus*," he inhales, his face pale and wan.

Almost twenty-eight years later and, when I let myself focus, the pain is as sharp as ever. I swallow it back, reminding myself that accidents happen. There was nothing anyone could have done. It wasn't my fault. Being there wouldn't have changed anything.

His fist hitting the table hard enough to make our glasses tremble and rattle has me jerking back in surprise. "I hate that you never said anything." His blue eyes are dark as he stares me down. "Not because I think I deserved to know, but because the idea of you suffering with this on your own…"

I don't argue with him because I understand. The urge to support and care for his friends is part of what underpins his natural drive to the Daddy lifestyle.

Instead, I sigh. "I've been to countless therapy sessions. I'm in support groups for grieving parents. I'm not on my own in this. I just…I don't want it spilling over into the life I built for myself *after*. My loss doesn't define me. And, Charlie," I add when it looks like he's still going to push the issue, "I'm okay. I promise."

And I am. Obviously, there will always be times that are harder than others, but I learned early on that if I didn't push forward and focus on the good things in my life, nothing was ever going to work again. And, once I changed my motivations for seeking out Daddy role play from focusing on proving that I could nurture and support someone to embracing my natural desire to do so, it made stumbling into the lifestyle as a grieving twenty-year-old a bit less weird.

As if he can read my mind, my friend sighs heavily and says, "You know that, if this thing between you and Zephyr gets serious, you'll have to tell him."

I reel back a little at that. I've never told any of my partners about Aiden. It's not that I can't see how it *might* be relevant, but I keep the two parts of my life completely separate. Before and After.

Reading my reluctance on my face, Charlie pushes it further. "If only to prevent a triggering event, or—"

I hold up my hand, interrupting him. "I see where you're coming from," I answer slowly. "But I'm asking you to drop it…and to keep this just between us."

That last bit might be asking a lot, but I don't want my relationship with the rest of our friendship circle changing, either. Still, I'm the one who taught Charlie about the importance of open and honest communication being paramount in a Daddy/Little relationship (or, really, any relationship). I can tell he's unimpressed at my request, but I don't back down.

His lips thin as he purses them, and I can practically see him wanting to remind me of the things I've said before. However, I've been at this for almost three decades and, as far as I'm concerned, my past has never had an impact on the success or subsequent failures of my relationships to date.

"I know what I'm doing," I insist. "I'm fine."

And I really do believe that.

Chapter Ten – Zephyr

Dating Ted is like a revelation. We spend the first month settling into routines. We both work full time, and I still enjoy a bit of time to myself in my own personal space, so we talk during the week and spend Friday nights through to Monday mornings together.

When we're apart, I don't feel the need to be little, so our calls and texts are like any standard vanilla relationship I've had before, except with a bit of kink thrown in for flirting. But, in person, Ted makes sure we've got a set routine in place. He's not big on surprises and likes control, which I can understand and even relate to, so it's not a big deal to know that I can expect scheduled times for being little.

That said, Ted is a bit more fluid once I've sunk into Little space, not minding if we go over the few hours an evening he allocates for it. I think he just likes me to know that he's making it a priority for the both of us, considering it's something we only explore together in person.

Tonight, though, things hit a snag.

It's like a switch is flipped the second I attempt to bring his hand to my cock during bath time, with me in the tub and him on his knees beside it, bathing me while I remain little for longer than anticipated. It's a Friday evening, and I'm gearing up for a weekend spent in bed if I can get my way.

Ted goes rigid, his face turning blank, and I don't even get a chance to speak before he clearly says, "Red light."

It's been a long time since I've safe worded myself, and I've never had a Daddy safe word with me, so I freeze and come back to my adult self so suddenly that it almost feels like I've given my brain whiplash. He's pulled his arm away from the tub, sitting back on his haunches, and I fight the sudden anxiety churning in my gut for having accidentally pushed a button.

I've called him 'Daddy' during sex before, but he's been okay with that. It has to be that I'm little right now. I run back through our conversations and negotiations and realize with a sinking feeling that, somehow, the topic of sex in Little space never even came up. That's on both of us.

This is why safe words exist, I remind myself, willing my heart to calm as I try to find the words to fix the strained silence that has descended.

"Hey," I reach for him, not caring about the water that drips from my bubble covered hand and onto the floor in front of his knees. "I'm sorry I..."

"No," he gives himself a visible shake, his expression turning chagrined. "I'm sorry. I should have..." He trails off and scratches the back of his neck, exhaling heavily. "That's a hard limit for me. One I should have raised earlier. It's just...most men I've been with haven't..."

"Wanted sex while little?" I prompt. It makes more sense now that he seems to easily ignore my arousal when he's dressing me: it's not on his radar. Little time is pure for him. I can respect that.

He nods.

"Want to talk about it?"

The vehement shake of his head in the negative begins before I can even finish asking the question. Something tells me this is a bigger deal than just disliking the concept. Ted's usually big on talking things through, with communication and honesty being at the top of our rules and all, so this flat refusal absolutely floors me.

Still, I know better than anyone not to push on uncomfortable or painful subjects. I have to trust that whatever's going on with him, Ted will talk to me when he's ready.

"Okay," I answer softly again, as though I'm trying to coax a skittish animal into trusting me. "That's fine. There are things I don't like talking about, either."

My easy acceptance seems to help, even while my mind races. What could have inspired this sort of reaction in a man who I was starting to think is always stoic and strong? Past trauma, certainly. But with what? Or whom? Another Little? Even though the Daddy/boy kink is pretty pure, it is still a facet of BDSM and people have all sorts of triggers. It's possible something went terribly wrong somewhere along the lines.

I climb out of the tub and dry myself off, the mood between us awkward and strained. I don't know how to make it better, and the last thing I want is for safe wording to feel...well, unsafe, for lack of a better word.

"Ice cream?" I suggest as brightly as I can as I pull my loose pajama pants up my legs. "And a movie?" I force a grin that I know doesn't quite meet my eyes. "You can even pick the movie...but I'm vetoing anything with Kevin Costner on principal."

Finally, I watch him relax. His eyes glint with humor. "What's wrong with—"

"Dude can't act, Ted. He just can't. It's painful to watch."

"But—"

"I will give you *Robin Hood: Prince of Thieves* but only because Alan Rickman carries that whole movie."

He snorts. We've had some variation of this argument before, but I'll happily rehash it if it means watching him smile and come back to himself after whatever the fuck just happened between us. "Next you'll tell me that the first *Die Hard* movie is the best one for the same reason."

"Well, duh," I laugh at his scandalized expression. "Actually, that would probably be unfair to Jeremy Irons in the third one, but…what can I say? I'm a Rickmaniac."

"A…*what*?" Ted stops in his tracks just as we're about to descend the stairs. He looks bewildered – clearly amused and also mildly horrified. "Is that like a Cumberbitch?"

"Ooooh," I tease him back, "Look who's up with the lingo. And you try to pretend you're middle-aged." I pat his shoulder and he sets off down the stairs in front of me. "You're secretly all over the celebrity gossip and stuff, aren't you?"

"You've got me," he deadpans, "I'm totally hip."

"Hip replacement maybe."

We've reached the bottom of the stairs and I squeal as he makes a swipe for me, playfully threatening retribution for the wise crack against his age. I race for the kitchen, laughing and breathless when he catches up to me, cornering me against the kitchen bench and kissing me senseless.

"I really am sorry about earlier," he says as we pull apart, his eyes meeting mine so I can gauge his sincerity. "It's my fault for not listing it in my limits."

"Honestly, it's fine." I reach up to cup his jaw in my palm, stroking my thumb over the prickle of a day's growth. "And when —*if*— you want to talk about it, we can. But it's enough just to know that you're not into it."

This time when Ted kisses me, I can't help but feel like he's trying to apologize anyway. He's tender and sweet and appreciative, and when he rests his forehead against mine afterwards, murmuring, "How'd I get so lucky with you, tiny dancer?" my insides light up.

It's only been a month, but I can feel myself falling for this man. It's a new sensation. I've been smitten before, and I've loved before, but nothing has felt quite this intense so quickly. I don't feel like we're rushing things, but at the same time, I'm surprised by how fast my feelings have progressed.

In past relationships, my feelings have been slow to build. I had to work hard on building the foundations before I got so attached. But with Ted I think I was attached from the beginning. He draws me in like nobody I've ever met before, and the foundations (the friendship and the flirting and the things we have in common) all seem to click into place without any actual effort.

Coming back to the conversation at hand, I smile and wrap my arms around his neck. "I'd say you're not the only one who hit the jackpot, Mister Masters."

"Is that so?" With his smile turning wicked, the remnants of our earlier tension begin to melt away.

"Uh huh. See, I've got this insanely hot silver fox at my disposal...and he's going to feed me ice cream and treat me like a queen."

Even though I've said it playfully, that's exactly how the

evening plays out.

* * *

By the time Wednesday rolls around, I've pretty much forgotten all about Friday's incident when I meet up with Asher for lunch. Their community center is only a fifteen-minute walk from the dance studio where I teach, so Ash and I have made this a regular event since we met, with Charlie tagging along with his husband when he's not in meetings.

I have to admit, it has been good making new friends. When I first came to the city, I was still trying to adjust to my new reality, and I'd been content with the idea of being a lone wolf. All my dance friends had moved on with their lives, keeping in touch via memes on Facebook, but never really stopping to ask how I was actually doing. It hurt too much to watch them continue with their careers, and eventually I just gave up the pretense. It was easier to be alone than to carry on with fair weather friends.

I hadn't been looking for a new social circle when I went to The Grove that first time. I really had just been looking for a bit of escapism and being little usually helped with that.

Then I'd met Ash and Chance.

Ash, for all that he tries to tell me that he's painfully shy, saw that I was alone and demanded that I play with him. He got me to open up about being new to town and somehow sensed how lonely I was, but never made me feel badly for it. He just told me that he had also started from scratch a couple of years ago and that he was always looking to make new friends. There was no sense of expectation from him, just his genuine joy at sharing his Little time with a playmate.

Once they'd explained that Chance wasn't Ash's Daddy but was stepping in as Uncle Chance, he had sat back and just let us play, occasionally joining in whenever Ash prodded him. Of the two of them, he's the one that struck me as genuinely shy, though he was every bit a doting Daddy when it was required of him. Afterwards, when Ash and I had gotten changed and were 'big' again, we'd all walked together to our cars, laughing and chatting like we were old friends.

It had struck me in that moment that being a loner would never work for me, and when Ash had suggested we exchange numbers, I couldn't deny that building a new social circle sounded appealing.

Since then, I've gotten pretty close with my fellow Little. Being strong-armed into attending his wedding was a surprise, but I'm beyond glad that I went along. At the time, I suspected he was trying to set me up with Chance because we had gotten along during Littles' Night, but now I realize that he was just trying to introduce me to their entire group. The fact that I ended up hitting it off with Ted is, to Ash, the cherry on top.

When I first confirmed that we were dating, he squealed, added me to the group chat, and started planning play-dates. Today he's brought Charlie with him and I anticipate more of the same, but when Ash brings it up because we are still yet to make it happen, Charlie frowns.

That sets off a bubble of anxiety in my gut.

"What's wrong?" I prod, running a fry through a small puddle of ketchup, my appetite fading the more I look at Charlie's face.

He attempts to school his expression into something milder. "Nothing," he says, shrugging casually. "I'll run it by Ted."

I don't know Charlie as well as I know Ash, but there's something *off* about the way he says his best friend's name.

"Have you guys argued?" I hazard a guess, watching Charlie closely for his reaction.

I'll give it to him; he's pretty cool under pressure, probably because he was a cop. But his eyes are expressive and they give him away. I can tell he's uneasy, even while he blinks slowly to control his facial expressions. "Nope."

Liar. I want to call him out on it, but at the same time I don't think it's really my place to do so. Whatever's going on between him and Ted, it probably has nothing to do with me. Besides, we haven't been together long enough for me to reasonably stick my nose in where it doesn't belong.

Ash, on the other hand, has no such compulsions. He cocks his head at his husband and says, "Want to try that again?"

"Ash…" The word is essentially a plea for Asher to let it go.

Proving that we're very similar people, Ash only digs his heels in. He sets down his fork, abandoning the creamy pasta dish he'd ordered, and glares at the other man. "What happened to honesty and open communication, Daddy? Do you have a problem with Ted and Zephyr together? Because I've been begging you to invite them over for weeks now and you've made excuse after excuse."

"What? No." That, at least, is an honest reaction. Charlie shakes his head, sighing. "Look. Ted and I…things there are a bit strained right now, okay? But it doesn't have anything to do with Zephyr." He shoots me an apologetic grimace. "I'm sorry if it came off that way."

"So you did fight with him?" Ash's face falls. "When? Why didn't you say anything?"

"It wasn't a fight," Charlie insists. "We just had an emotionally charged conversation and things are still a bit weird right now. I'm giving him time and space."

Hearing the confirmation doesn't really help me. If anything, it makes me more anxious because Ted never mentioned having a falling out with his friend to me, either. Ash and I exchange uneasy glances.

"Just forget I said anything, okay?" Charlie insists. "Please. He…" he sighs, then looks at his husband imploringly, "We're good, okay? Just…he asked me to back off and drop it, and I am. So…can you leave it? Please?"

Pursing his lips, Ash nods with obvious reluctance. "Fine."

In his relief, Charlie does not catch the look Ash shoots me, but I obviously do. And I nod, because there's no way we're not getting to the bottom of whatever is going on between our Daddies.

Chapter Eleven – Ted

"Oh, God, *Zeph*," his beautiful bow lips are wrapped around my cock and I'm finding it very difficult to form coherent thoughts right now.

We've disposed of condoms recently, having both tested negative for STIs, and the warm, wet suction of his mouth makes that particular decision one of my finest.

He bobs his head, swirling his tongue over my shaft and through the slit of my crown as he moves.

"You feel so good, darling," I encourage him further, trying not to tighten my fingers in his thick, dark hair.

I'm sprawled on the couch in my living room, my legs spread wide with Zephyr kneeling between them. My jeans have been thrown somewhere in the direction of the kitchen. The only reason I give two shits about that right now is the sachet of lube stashed in my wallet which is still in the hip pocket of said jeans.

Zephyr hums, sending vibrations through my cock and pushing me ever closer to orgasm.

My brain turns sluggish. "Wait, baby…I— *oh fuck,* that feels… *ungh.*"

I throw my head back against the plush couch cushion and close my eyes, reveling in the feel of him sucking me off. He smooths his hands over my thighs and then fondles my balls with one while the other dips lower, grazing my taint and teasing my hole.

My hips buck upwards of their own accord as I groan my enjoyment.

Then I remember that my intention is to not come down his throat.

"Zeph…lube. Wallet." I used to have the ability to form sentences, I swear.

"Mmm," he moans around my cock again, and it's all I can do to keep my eye on the prize. Then he pulls off and asks, "Is the lube for your ass or mine?"

Fun fact: I've never been fucked. I've had my ass played with, sure, but none of my boys have wanted to top, and I've never felt as though I've been missing out. In fact, until ten seconds ago, I would have told you I'm a strict top. But what comes out of my mouth is: "Is that something you'd want to do? Fuck me, I mean?"

Zephyr blinks at me in surprise, the blow job all but forgotten. "I've never topped."

I shrug easily. "I've never bottomed."

His eyes are wide now, his disbelief almost palpable. "But… you'd let me…?"

Reaching for him, I pull him up into my lap and kiss his swollen lips. "I trust you," I tell him simply. "My previous partners haven't been interested in topping, and I never pushed the issue. But if you want to try, I'm always up for experimentation." I waggle my eyebrows to keep the mood light. "It doesn't have to be today, or ever if you don't want to, but I'd be on board if you wanted it."

"Wow," he says, those dark eyes of his glazing over. "That is *hot*, Ted."

I think about it for a moment, imagining what he might feel like inside me, and my cock twitches between us at the thought. "Yeah," I agree, the heat and urgency from a few minutes ago building between us again, "it is."

He mewls and then crashes his lips against mine, kissing me with fervent need. My hands move to the fly of his jeans, popping the button and undoing the zipper with practiced ease. We fumble and shift around as he struggles his way out of them while our tongues tangle together, our breaths mingling and our mutual desire growing.

"Fuck," he hisses, breaking from the kiss when our cocks connect, both a little slick with precum, "where'd you say the lube was?"

I groan again, this time in frustration. "In my wallet. In my jeans." I gesture in the vague direction I saw them fly earlier. "Wherever they went."

"Ugh. Fine." He climbs off my lap with obvious reluctance. "Be right back."

"I'll be waiting." I fist my cock for emphasis.

I don't bother watching as he races in the direction of the kitchen, but I hear his victorious "Got it!" and the dull sound of the denim hitting the tiles before he's back in front of me again, the small square pouch of lube extended in one hand.

"For now," he says with a grin, "you're going to fuck me. But one day, we'll switch it up."

"Anything you want, Zeph." And I mean it. I want to give

him the world.

But today I'll settle for a mind-blowing orgasm or two.

He straddles my lap again, kissing me as I manage to awkwardly tear open the little packet and coat my fingers. I take my time opening him up as he grinds his cock against mine, stretching him with three fingers before I deem him ready enough to ride me. I squeeze the last of the lube out into my palm and slick up my cock, then guide Zephyr until he's sinking down onto me in one smooth, swift move.

"Holy fuck," I breathe and dig my fingers into his hips. As always, the sensation of being inside him is beyond exquisite, even more so now that we've agree to go bare. "I'll never get used to how good you feel."

Using muscles toned from a lifetime of dancing, he starts to bounce in my lap, his knees on either side of my ass, sinking into the couch. "Right back at you," he says between movements, closing his eyes as my cock grazes over his prostate. "Oh, *Daddy.*"

"That's it, baby. Take it. Take what you need."

I love watching him like this. Love feeling him use me for his own pleasure. It's so different to have someone else set the pace, to hand the reins over to someone else and let them control the experience, but it's also surprisingly freeing. And watching Zephyr this way, knowing that he's comfortable enough to take whatever he needs from me, fills me with pride, warmth, and affection.

"T-touch my cock," he stammers out as he finds the angle and pace guaranteed to have him hurtling over the finish line before too long. "Please."

As if I need to be begged for that. My hand closes around his length, stroking and squeezing the way he likes best, and he begins his usual litany of curses as the pleasure builds.

I focus on him. On his blissed-out expression. On the sheen of sweat on his skin. On the precum dribbling down his cock, aiding my hand's endeavors. On the panted out swear words and the sounds of him taking his pleasure from me. On the slapping sound of skin meeting skin as he rides me with wild abandon.

I'm rocking my hips up to meet him with every bounce and it's not long before the swears turn into the tell-tale train of fast cussing that precipitates his whole body tensing and ropes of cum spurting over my fist and our shirts. As always, he clenches around my cock as he comes and I'm unable to prevent myself from releasing my own load inside him.

We're a sticky, panting, practically glowing mess as we come down from the high of our mutual orgasms, but Zephyr makes no move to pull off me, not even as I start to soften. He drops his head to my shoulder and kisses my neck.

"I swear," he declares with a smile in his voice, "every time we do that, I think I'm going to black out with how hard you make me come."

"You did all the hard work this time, kitten," I remind him lazily, rubbing my clean hand over his back.

The sound he responds with is non-committal.

With reluctance, I tap his bare ass with my open palm. "Come on," I tell him, "Let's go clean up."

* * *

After an extended shower, Zephyr locates his phone and offers me a wide smile as he holds it up. "Are we going?" he asks, practically bouncing on his feet. I frown.

"Are we going where?"

"To Ash and Charlie's place," he points at the phone screen, "they've invited us all around for an impromptu cookout. It's in the group chat."

I muted the group chat weeks ago. It's not uncommon for me to need to do so occasionally. It is a large group which is becoming even larger with everyone's partners being read in, and they talk a lot of crap sometimes. The sheer number of notifications can be ridiculous and distracting when I'm at work. The guys, including Cherie and Kate, are generally accepting of the fact that I miss most of the conversations and don't participate a lot.

But I didn't mute the chat for work reasons this time.

After talking to Charlie about my past, I gave myself a time-out from the chat. I trust that he hasn't told any of the others, not even Ash. If he had, I would have been inundated with calls or messages, because our group is meddlesome like that.

Not that I don't think they'd all be supportive and kind, mind you. Because they would be. They're wonderful people. But I don't want our dynamic to change. I don't want their pity, or for things to become stilted or awkward.

Like they have with Charlie.

It hurts that my closest friend and I aren't exactly speaking right now. And, alright: I asked him to drop it and to give me space and he's done just that, so I should be grateful. Besides, it's not as though we fought. Sure, Charlie's got a right to feel a touch hurt or insulted that I never confided in him, but he needs to be able to understand that I had my reasons and that it's my right to keep my personal issues…well, personal.

"Ted?" Zephyr's voice interrupts my thoughts and I look up to see his brow furrowed, his perfectly manicured eyebrows drawing down together.

While I'm tempted to tell him no, I can't come up with a valid reason to refuse Charlie and Ash's invitation. Then there's his obvious excitement at the prospect of socializing more with the whole gang. If it's a large enough gathering, I suppose it's possible that I can just avoid the awkwardness with Charlie altogether.

I twist my left wrist to check the time and smother a sigh. "What time is everyone getting there?"

Zephyr's expression morphs into surprise and then joy. "Six," he says, then his thumbs fly over the keypad on his screen, "I'm telling them we'll bring dessert."

I chuckle genuinely at that, at least. My princess and his sweet tooth. "Sure," I acknowledge. We don't really have time to bake anything, so I suggest a trip to the local bakery. I know I'm going to wind up buying far more than just sweet treats for tonight, but I can't help spoiling Zephyr and he knows it.

It's not until we're buckled into my car with a selection of pastries and cakes boxed and settled on the backseat that the anxiety I pushed aside earlier returns. Oblivious, Zephyr babbles about Ash's plan to host a play-date at the same time: the reason why Zephyr's packed himself a bag of his Little stuff for the evening.

"He said his friend Kate will be there, and so will Matt, and maybe even Josh might want to join in," he tells me, twisting in his seat to face me as he rambles with obvious excitement. "I haven't told him that I'm femme, but he'll be okay with it, right?"

I tear my eyes from the road briefly to assure him, "Of course. They all will. They're good guys."

That's not something I would ever question. My reluctance

to tell them about my past and about my loss has nothing to do with a fear of judgment, at least. If anything, I don't want their sympathy. I don't want them to treat me differently. I'm still the same Ted I've always been but, if Charlie's reaction is anything to go by, they're not going to see it that way.

Zephyr nods, seemingly accepting my words at face value. But, as silence descends upon us, he places his hand on my thigh and squeezes, "Are you okay?"

Maybe he's not quite as oblivious to my anxiety as I thought.

Not wanting to lie to him, I mull over how to respond. "I'm… just thinking."

"About?"

I should have known that question was coming.

I sigh, keeping my gaze firmly on the road ahead. "The last time I spoke to Charlie, I told him something that…" I trail off.

How do I express this?

I don't want Zephyr to worry, obviously, but I also don't need him learning about the shadows in my past, either, no matter what Charlie thinks.

"That…?" he prompts.

I make a turn in the familiar direction of Charlie's place. We're still about five minutes away. Not short enough that I could feasibly brush Zephyr off. "Well," I answer, still trying to verbalize my issue with as many euphemisms as feasibly possible, "I think it changed the way he sees me."

"Oh."

Belatedly, I can see how that explanation could be interpreted in a thousand different ways – not many of them pleasant.

"I mean," I try to reassure him, "it was something from a long time ago, something I've worked through, and I don't want him pitying me or treating me with kid gloves."

While I don't love that I've had to confess that there's something pitiable in my past, I'd rather Zephyr know that than assume I'd said or done something terrible.

From the corner of my eye, I can see my boyfriend's gaze narrowing while he tries to put the vague clues together. "Do you really think he'll pity you?" he asks, and I catch the shake of his head before he answers himself, "Charlie doesn't seem the type. He's pragmatic. He might *empathize* with you, but he doesn't come off the pitying type. And as for treating you differently—"

"He already is," I huff, feeling much younger and more vulnerable than my actual age. The fact that I asked Charlie for space is something I conveniently choose to forget as I make my point. "We haven't spoken in over a month. Things are awkward now."

Instead of comforting me, Zephyr pats my thigh. "Well, the only way to fix that is to talk to him, you know."

Now it's my turn to frown. He doesn't seem at all surprised at my confession that I haven't been in touch with my best friend recently. Almost like he already…

It clicks.

"Asher," I say aloud, mildly frustrated.

Ash and Zeph have spoken about this. About me and Charlie. Hell, for all I know, today's supposedly 'impromptu' get-together is part of a plot to resolve whatever issues they think are between us.

"Don't be mad…" Zephyr has the decency to shift guiltily in his seat.

If I weren't driving, I'd close my eyes and count to ten. Instead, I flex my hold on the wheel and take a deep breath.

"What did you and Ash do?"

"Nothing!" The quick, defensive reply sets off all my internal Daddy alarms.

"*Zephyr…*"

"I mean, we just thought that if you guys got together—"

I groan, cutting him off. I was right: this whole thing tonight has been a setup.

I've been Parent Trapped.

Unwilling to snap at him, because he really did mean well, I shake my head and indicate to turn onto Ash and Charlie's street. "You should have let it be," I manage to keep my tone level.

Zephyr remains silent.

As we approach Charlie's house and I pull up on the curb behind Chance's truck, I bite back further irritation that the guys are all here. Nothing like having an audience for tense moments. Turning in my seat to face my errant boy, I'm unsurprised to see the flat expression on his face, complete with pursed lips and folded arms.

"Zeph," I reach for him, but he leans back against the passenger window.

"Ash and I did what we thought was right," he insists, meeting my gaze unflinchingly. "You and Charlie weren't making any moves to get past whatever went down between you." His shoulders droop. "And I really wanted to have a play-date with my friend. A real one – not just at the club."

It's times like this where I'm reminded of his Little side. Zephyr acted on impulse, not even thinking about the implications of his and Asher's scheme, or how inviting the whole gang might make me feel.

Nevertheless, guilt still lances through me at his softly

spoken admission. *Damn it.* It hasn't been fair of me to keep him all to myself for so long. Sure, part of that was all the shiny new relationship feelings and exploration, but I can't deny that avoiding Charlie was also a great motivator.

"You're right," I acknowledge, even though doing so is difficult. "I'm sorry, tiny dancer. I've been selfish."

Zephyr's expression softens. "I'm sorry, too. I shouldn't have just sprung this on you. I should have just spoken to you about it. And we probably shouldn't have made it a whole group thing, but we didn't want it to look like a setup…" He turns his gaze towards the house, then back to me. "If you'd rather go home, we can do that."

It's tempting, and I do appreciate the offer, but I've let this strange limbo with my closest friend go on for too long as it is. "No," I state softly, but firmly. "I need to do this."

I don't deserve the look of pride he gives me in response, but it warms me anyway.

Chapter Twelve – Zephyr

Ash and Charlie's house is lovely. From the street, it gives off a pretty cottage vibe. It's two stories, constructed out of light gray clapboard with white accents and a nice front porch complete with a flowerbed full of brightly colored flowers. It's homey and inviting and (though I hate to think it) far less intimidating than Ted's mansion.

As we walk in —with Ted just opening the front door and sauntering through without ringing the bell— the same color scheme continues inside. Ted leads me through the small foyer and past an office and staircase on my left and a carpeted lounge room on my right. When we get into an open plan kitchen/dining area which leads further on to an outdoor entertainment space, Ash notices us first. He steps away from Kate and Matt, both of whom I met at his wedding, and bounds over to greet us.

"Hey, Uncle Ted," he grins, wrapping his arms around my Daddy before turning to me, "Hey, Zephyr. I'm so happy you could come!"

I can't help smiling back in the face of his genuine enthusiasm. "Me too," I agree.

Ted, on the other hand, gives Ash a stern look.

I sigh, explaining, "We've been busted."

Ash turns back to Ted and shrugs. "We gave you and Daddy long enough to sort your shit out. You didn't do it on your own so," he spreads his arms wide, "here we are. Sorry not sorry, Ted."

"Actually," I interrupt before Ted can scold my friend. Having had the discussion with Ted and gotten a very vague idea of what happened between him and Charlie, I do feel guilty for just springing this intervention of sorts on him, "we're a bit sorry."

Ash furrows his brow. "We are?"

"We are." I give him a meaningful look. One that says 'I'll tell you later'.

"Hmm," is all my fellow Little says before he turns back in the direction of the gathering out on the deck, "*Daddy,*" he calls cheerily before anyone can stop him, "Ted and Zephyr are here!"

I can feel Ted tense beside me and I reach out to rub at the underside of his arm (which is holding the large box of pastries and doughnuts) to soothe him.

"Here," chirps Ash helpfully, "I'll take those." Following through, he plucks the box of desserts out of Ted's hands and bounces into the kitchen.

Charlie makes his way inside, his hand extended to shake mine before he looks at his best friend. There's a brief, strained moment of silence between them before Charlie hauls Ted in for a manly hug, all back thumping and "I've missed you, man, how've you been?"s.

Ash and I share a relieved glance as the two men lapse into conversation from there. To be fair, it's probably not the easy and effortless conversations they usually share, and I can still see tension in the way Ted holds his shoulders. But it's a start.

"Come on," Ash grabs my hand and starts leading me towards the other Littles in the gathering, "we're thinking about getting changed and having a play-date." He juts his chin at the duffel bag slung over my shoulder. "Is that your Little stuff?"

I nod. "Yeah." Now it's my turn to feel nervous. I know Ted said nobody here will judge me for being into feminization, but…*what if they do?*

We've stopped in front of Kate and Matt, and Ash is leading the discussion on whether they're interested in sneaking in some Little time before dinner or not when Charlie's brother, Josh, joins the party. His entrance is boisterous, and he, too, appears to have just let himself into the house. As he enters the room, he waves at the people gathered outside before making a beeline towards his brother-in-law.

"Thanks for the invite, Ash," he says, ruffling the smaller man's hair. Then he looks over the rest of us. "So, are we doing this? Getting our Little on?"

"Where's your stuff?" Ash asks him. "Or are you staying in what you're wearing?"

He glances down at the white t-shirt and jeans combination he's rocking and shrugs. "I'm easy."

"There's a joke in that," Chance teases, happening to walk past us at that moment. Josh flips him off, and the other man grabs two beers from the fridge with a laugh before returning to the group of caregivers outside.

Ash rolls his eyes at the exchange, then looks Josh over again. "Suit yourself," he says, then adds, "but I know I can't really get into the right head space if I'm wearing my 'big' clothes."

"I've got a spare set of clothes if you wanted to borrow an outfit," Matt offers him. He's a bit bulkier than Josh up top, but I'd guess they're roughly around the same size.

Josh looks at Matt for a long moment, likely considering the offer, then smiles hesitantly. I don't really know the guy, having only met him at Ash's wedding, but from everything Ash has told me about him, such an expression seems almost out of place on his handsome face. "Thanks, Matt," he says to the other buff Little, "I'd like that."

And, just like that, it seems to be decided that the play-date will start as soon as we're all changed. Matt shyly seeks out London to take him to one of the guest rooms and dress him, and Katie drags her Mommy, Cherie, up the stairs after them to do the same. Charlie doesn't need prompting, he just heads towards the stairs with Ash on his heels. This leaves me to consider whether I want to ask Ted to help me, or whether I should just head into the downstairs powder room to dress myself. It's not like I need diapering or anything like the others.

Of course, I haven't warned them about my dresses, either.

"Hey," Josh's voice startles me out of my thoughts. His brown eyes are concerned. "You okay?"

It's in this moment that I realize that his brazen personality must be a façade, because, if memory serves correctly, the guy is a cop. And this serious, concerned manner he's got going on right now? It's genuine.

His voice is soft, and he reaches out a hand to squeeze my shoulder. "If you're not up for this, we can grab drinks and go join the other guys."

I've only met this guy once, but the way he so easily offers to sit out on Little time to keep me company warms me unexpectedly. I smile and shake my head, even as Ted sidles up beside Josh, eyeing his hand on my shoulder with unspoken questions.

"Zeph?" Ted asks, his own concern more than obvious.

"I'm fine," I reassure both men, leaning into Ted's side when Josh releases his hold on my shoulder. Then I sigh and heft my bag up as I explain, "I didn't get a chance to tell the others."

"Tell the others what?" Josh asks, but he doesn't sound demanding. Just curious. Still gentle and supportive.

It's his tone and the open look on his face which ultimately convince me to admit, "I'm into feminization. I'm, uh, a femme Little. Like, y'know, princess play and pretty dresses and… stuff." I finish lamely.

A wide, bright smile splits his face. "Katie is going to lose her shit." He claps his hands together. "*And* that means I don't have to play dress-ups with her anymore!" He lunges forward, wrapping me in a bear hug. He stops shy of spinning me around in his joy. "You're my hero!" When he sets me back down on the ground, he offers me a bashful smile. "I mean, dress-ups aren't the worst, but they're not my jam."

I can't help but think he's sweet to have still gone along with it all this time for his friend. Ted was right: these are good people. I'm safe here.

I turn back to my Daddy, my worries alleviated. "Wanna help me get dressed?"

* * *

Despite knowing that Ted's friends are good people and that I'm safe, I still clutch Ted's hand tightly as we make our way back downstairs to rejoin the group. I'm wearing a dress which

Ted bought me last week. It's a very pale pink color, with a flared skirt that sits just above my knees, a fitted bodice, and spaghetti straps over my shoulders. It's perfect and summery and I feel supremely feminine wearing it. The matching ballet flats I'm wearing complete the whole picture.

"It's going to be fine, kitten," Ted assures me, bringing my hand to his mouth and brushing his lips lightly over my knuckles. "I promise."

I can't really explain why I'm so anxious about this, other than the fact that it's the first time a group of people I know will see me dressed this way. Ash and Chance have seen me in a cropped t-shirt and play shorts, but this is different. This is me laid bare. And that's what it ultimately boils down to: I really want them to like me for me.

As we cross the foyer and head towards the lounge room, finally coming into view of the others, I watch them closely for their first reactions before they have a chance to school their features.

It's only as Ash's face lights up that the tension starts to bleed from my shoulders. Matt smiles, too, but there's something softer and more understanding in his gaze. Then there's Kate, who squeals and rushes towards me, her arms extended in a bid to reach out and feel the material of my dress before she's even crossed the space.

"*Finally,*" she gushes, sounding giddy. "Someone like me."

I don't know what it is about her words that do it, but I tear up at that very simple declaration. She doesn't see my gender: she just sees another Little who likes to wear pretty dresses.

Before I know it, Kate and I are hugging as though we've been friends for years instead of minutes, and then there's a dog pile of people on top of us with the other Littles wanting in on the embrace. It's not until minutes later, when we're all giggling and moving off to play, that I realize Ted wandered off to join Charlie over by the couch. Cherie and London, Kate's Mommy and Matt's Daddy respectively, are back out on the deck with Spencer and Chance.

If I were in a bigger head space, I'd probably pay closer attention to the low-spoken conversation my Daddy is having with his best friend, but I'm too distracted by Kate's request to play dolls with me.

Even though I've played with dolls before (by myself, in scenes at various clubs, and more recently with Ted as my very attentive Daddy) I discover that having a Little friend to play with is a whole new experience. She's every bit as enthusiastic as I am, losing herself in the imaginative play.

While Daddy joins in in a similar way, he's never quite as invested as Kate seems to be. He doesn't share the childlike glee that she and I feel, I suppose. And why should he? He's a *Daddy*, not a fellow Little. His enjoyment comes from interacting with me and seeing me happy. Whereas, for Kate and I, our enjoyment as Littles comes from letting go of being adults. Of letting someone else take care of us while we give in to the urge to be completely carefree.

When we get bored of playing dolls, Kate and I move on to orchestrating a pretend tea party for them. We just dressed them up, after all. It makes sense that they should have a reason to wear their 'fancy' new outfits. Ash ambles over for this game, though, and I vaguely recall Ted telling me that Ash loves to play teddy bear tea parties.

Matt and Josh stick to racing their cars along the polished timber floorboards separating the lounge from the kitchen.

Our caregivers leave us to our own devices, though occasionally one of the caregivers will stop in to ask questions or join our play for a few minutes. I don't even realize how much time has passed when Charlie wanders back into the room having swapped out 'watching' us with Spencer to go fiddle with the grill on the deck, and he claps his hands, declaring dinner ready.

"You can stay little if you want," he says easily, as though this sort of thing happens every day, "but we should eat it before it gets cold." He chuckles and wraps an arm around Asher's waist, catching him as he tries to slip past. "But, big or little, you need to wash up first, too."

Ash grumbles, but the smile playing around the corners of his lips gives his enjoyment of this interaction with his Daddy away. Watching them like this fills me with warm, fuzzy feelings, and I fleetingly wonder if Ted and I ever look at each other the way Charlie and Ash do.

As I make my way to get changed back into my big clothes, a hopeful voice in my head says that if we don't already, I think we're on the right track.

Chapter Thirteen – Ted

I owe Zephyr an apology and gratitude for forcing me to face my issues with Charlie. The first few minutes of conversation felt a touch strained but, after sitting together and watching the Littles romp around Charlie's lounge room, we're back to our usual dynamic now, or a close approximation to it. And, as I take a seat at one of the two outdoor tables which have been pushed together to create one long one, I realize just how badly I've missed this.

I'm a social creature by nature. Not having hung out with the guys in over a month was more emotionally and mentally draining than I could have anticipated. Not only that, but I can see that Zephyr needed the social time just as badly as I did. While he was quite obviously anxious at first, I couldn't deny the blatant joy and relaxation he seemed to get from playing with the others as I watched indulgently.

Guilt wells in me, churning my gut when I consider that my avoidance of my friends also prevented Zephyr from having this sort of experience.

"Whatever you're thinking, man, stop it," Spencer says lowly as he leans across me to grab for a big bowl of green salad. "You've got your 'self-flagellation' face on." He dishes himself up a healthy serving of rabbit food before handing the bowl down the line to Chance.

On my other side, Zephyr's in quiet conversation with London, their heads bowed together as they murmur softly. With him distracted, I turn back to Spencer, repeating, "My self-flagellation face?"

He nods, his mess of dark hair flopping into his eyes. "It's not a good look on you."

I want to argue, but I can't deny that he's right. Of course, I can't help snarking, "Interesting way of phrasing it. What kind of books are you narrating right now?"

He reaches for some of the chicken Charlie had cooked on the grill and smirks at me as he returns the tongs to the plate. "No changing the subject, Theodore."

I roll my eyes. "You can't use Daddy voice on another Daddy, Spencer. We've been over this."

He continues on, undeterred, "Either way, whatever's making you second guess yourself? You gotta stop that." He jerks his chin towards Zephyr. "Your boy is sweet, and you've got a good thing going. Don't get so far into your head that you let it slip away."

I don't like how accurately he was able to read me in the short time we've been seated together at the table. But I also know that he hasn't dated since his relationship with Emma ended all those months ago, and now I'm coming to see that maybe he's not so much reading me as possibly projecting his own issues onto me.

My initial reaction to bristle and snap at him softens into

something a little more understanding. I even manage to sound mildly appreciative when I assure him, "Thanks, Spence. I won't let that happen."

Placing his knife down on his plate, he reaches up to squeeze my shoulder and gives me a soft shake before he lets go. "I'm glad."

Even though I was irritated at first, it's just another example of how good the guys in our circle of friends really are. They look out for each other, even on this smaller level. I feel like a shitty friend for not having returned the favor lately.

"You're doing it again," Spence says, cutting off my thoughts.

I give him a one-fingered salute.

He allows me a few moments of silence before he leans in and quietly asks, "Did you want to talk about it?"

"No." My reply is quick and emphatic.

Spencer's lips quirk. "You gave that a lot of thought."

"Fuck off," I laugh. "There's nothing to talk about."

Across the table, Charlie chokes on the sip of beer he'd only just taken. I narrow my gaze in his direction. Maybe we're not exactly as back to 'normal' as I'd hoped.

"Sorry," he coughs, his cheeks a little pink, but he doesn't push the issue.

Spencer arches an eyebrow at the exchange. I ignore it.

Thankfully, Ash asks Zephyr about the dress he'd worn earlier and Kate chimes in loudly from the other end of the table, and the whole awkward moment is forgotten.

* * *

Everything goes south when Maisy, Josh and Charlie's sister, turns up unexpectedly.

Having let herself into the house, most likely realizing that Ash and Charlie were entertaining, she stomps out onto the deck and practically throws herself into her older brother's arms.

"Mom's driving me *insane*," she complains, seemingly oblivious to the way silence has fallen around the table. "I finally snapped and told her that Ed and I have zero intention to have kids and she's acting like I've told her the world is ending."

Beside me, Spencer tenses. I don't have time to think about his reaction, though, because Maisy has worked herself up into a proper rant and raises her voice, her arms flailing about wildly. Idly, I muse that while she mightn't look like her mother, their shared dramatic flair is obviously genetic.

"She even said, and I quote: 'I did too good a job when I gave you *the talk*,'" she pitches her voice high in a mocking mimicry of her mother's voice. Her face contorts bitterly and she scoffs. "As if I was only careful for her benefit. Who wants to be a teen statistic? Or any kind of statistic? Unplanned kids aren't exactly—"

"*Maisy*," Charlie interrupts in his firmest voice, startling the whole table. Ash puts a calming hand on his arm, but he continues, "Your personal opinion on that stuff is irrelevant because it never happened and Mom's just being Mom right now."

I try not to cringe at the fleeting apologetic glance he shoots my way. What happened to Subtle Cop Charlie? *Come on, man,* I try to tell him with my eyes, *be cool.*

Maisy huffs and rolls her eyes. "I'm *venting*," she justifies emphatically, then waves her hand dismissively over the table. "It's not like any of these guys'll be offended or whatever."

"You don't know that." Charlie lectures back.

Again his eyes flicker in my direction.

Damn it, Charlie.

Maisy sighs. I can understand her likely assumptions without her needing to say anything out loud: we're a gathering of predominantly gay men, as far as she's aware. What, exactly, are the chances any of us were teen parents? However, to play devil's advocate, I would argue that we might have family or friends who were. (Unbeknownst to the guys, they've got at least one friend who was, after all.)

Still, it's obvious that she's come here directly after a volatile interaction with her mother and her words are reactionary. I don't know her well, but we've met enough times over the years to know that Maisy's not a cruel or judgmental person. I honestly wouldn't have given her words a second thought, but Charlie's making a big deal out of them and I can feel myself attempting to sink into my chair because I know why this is a trigger for him right now.

I'm the only person here who does.

And, because my seat is directly across from where Charlie is standing beside his sister, it's me she zeroes in on to try and illustrate her point. "Ted," she huffs, aiming her index finger into her older brother's chest, "tell him that you're not offended."

I breathe a little easier at the loophole. Had she asked me directly if I had a reason to be hurt by her words, that would have given me pause. But this is easy because it's not a lie. I smile softly. "I'm not offended."

Unfortunately, Charlie frowns and tilts his head sideways with mild disbelief tempering his tone, *"Ted."*

My heart begins beating rapidly in my chest because in every single imagined scenario from here, I don't know how to get out of this without having to tell the guys everything after all. Even meeting his gaze and reassuring him that I'm honestly not offended will bring more attention to the issue than should be required.

I work my jaw and eye him down, but it's too late and I know it.

Zephyr's hand lands on my tense forearm. "What's going on?" he asks softly, voicing the question I'm certain is on everyone's minds by now. But, instead of acknowledging the question, I cringe in my best friend's direction, wishing he hadn't pushed the issue.

"Damn it, Charlie," I growl the words I thought only moments ago, shaking my head, "you couldn't have left it?" I run a hand through my hair, my eyes still not leaving his. "I genuinely wasn't offended, by the way. You could have just taken my word for it."

His reply is laden with sarcasm, "I'm sorry for thinking about your feelings."

"I told you—"

His scoff cuts me off. "Yeah, well, maybe…" I watch him trail off, uneasy at the expression that crosses his face. His shoulders slump with resignation and a little embarrassment. "Maybe I was projecting." He averts his gaze, gruffly adding, "Sorry."

"A fine time to have that realization," I grumble, then sigh, silently cursing the fact that my best friend is so damn empathetic and cursing myself for avoiding properly talking the whole thing out with him when I had the chance.

"Ted…" With Charlie's own temper deflated, there's genuine remorse on his features and in his voice now.

I shake my head and say, "Don't worry about it."

What's done is done. Besides, steeling myself for the fallout is more important than listening to him apologize for…what, exactly? Caring too much? Can I honestly hold that against him?

Awkward silence descends before Maisy demands, "No, seriously, what the hell is going on with you two?" She flicks a perfectly manicured nail between me and Charlie, before her attention swings back to her older brother properly. Her long, pretty face contorts as she narrows her eyes at him. She seems concerned beneath her snark now, her worry for her older brother overriding her frustration. "Projecting what, exactly? Did you actually knock someone up in high school?"

Down the table, Josh chokes on his drink at her question, and I sigh.

"No," I answer on Charlie's behalf, rolling my eyes because even I know that he came out in his mid-teens. I don't stop to think, I don't take a breath, and I certainly don't look at anyone other than Maisy when I tell her, "*I* did."

Chapter Fourteen — Zephyr

The drive back to Ted's place is more strained than the drive to Charlie's was. I have no idea what to say after the bombs he dropped over that disastrous dinner. Guilt roils my belly, because the whole reason we even went there tonight was because Ash and I wanted to get our Daddies to clear the air.

Mission accomplished, my snarky inner voice sasses me.

Not. Helping.

I shift uncomfortably in my seat, trying to expel the memory of Ted's stony expression as he laid the whole story out for his friends and I before he carefully pushed back his chair and walked away from the table, barely sparing a glance behind him to see if I was following.

Of course I was following. I think the entire group wanted to follow him, but they seemed to know better. They stayed silent as we left the impromptu party, holding their burning questions behind eyes that burned with shock and concern. I managed to cast Ash a loaded glance, promising to talk soon without exchanging words, before chasing Ted down the front pathway towards his car, my mind reeling.

To think that Ted's been dealing with his loss and his grief alone for his entire life is heartbreaking. He did his best to assure us that he's got support. There are groups for parents who have lost their children, and he still sees a therapist on a monthly basis, but I can't stop thinking about how hard it must have been to keep such a monumental part of his life to himself. To not slip up and mention his kid once in all the years he's known the guys. *The effort of that alone…* I bite my lip at the thought.

"Did you want me to drop you off at your place?" Ted's voice startles me out of my thoughts before the question can register in my brain.

"Wait…what?" I give my head a shake, frowning at him. He's staring resolutely at the road, his knuckles white as he grips the wheel tighter than need demands. "My place?"

It doesn't compute. It's a Saturday night. I *always* spend Saturdays at his place. We have pancakes for breakfast on Sundays and…*oh*. Is this Ted telling me that he doesn't want that now? Because Ash and I wanted to help and some comedy of errors had him spilling his tragic life story to his friends? I can't help but feel a bit of indignant rage well up within me, smothering the guilt I was feeling only minutes ago, despite some reasonable part of me knowing that he has every right to be upset with the role I played in this.

Ted's shoulders lift and drop, but he remains tight-lipped. I can see his jaw is tense, too.

"You don't want me to stay tonight?" I had hoped to keep my voice firm and strong, defiant in the face of his sour mood, but even I catch the wobble to it when the words leave my lips.

His Adam's apple bobs, but he doesn't turn his head to look at me, still feigning focus on the road. "I…" he trails off.

His reticence to answer gives me hope. If he really didn't want me to stay with him, he would have said as much.

Some of my anger fades as rapidly as it built, and I start to think rationally again, observing Ted closely.

I mightn't have known him long, but considering the nature of our relationship, I like to think I know him well now. And, on close inspection, I can see that my Daddy is tired. Stressed. Upset. But he's a proud man. An insanely independent man. And I'm his boy. Asking anything of me, especially something as huge as sticking around to support him through something tough, has got to be difficult for him.

For all his talk about open communication and honesty, this has been a blow to him. I don't feel like he's misled me in any way, but for his carefully hidden secrets (which I never assumed a right to know) to have come out the way they did will have hurt his pride and opened a wound that he was convinced was scarred over.

Then another revelation hits me.

I think back to that night not so long ago where I accidentally stumbled on his one hard limit, and it makes so much sense now. Knowing that he had a son adds an element to the Daddy/boy thing that I can't really ignore. No wonder he's got zero interest in sexual interactions when I'm little: his being a Daddy is *only* about nurture, possibly even a bit of unconscious guilt. How could I not have seen that before?

"I don't want to go back to my place, Ted." This time my voice is strong and definitive.

He's quiet for a stretch longer than is comfortable, but he nods. "Okay."

Tense silence falls over us again, broken only by the muted white noise of the tires against the road's surface and other traffic sounds. I rack my brain for the right words for the entire drive, still not sure what, if anything, I should say to him.

Even as we make our way from the garage, through the laundry and past the kitchen, neither one of us speaks. I can feel the intermittent vibration of my phone in my pocket that I've come to associate with the group chat, but I don't dare pull it out to read the chain of messages. I imagine that I already know what they'll say: nothing but support for Ted and assurance that they'll be there to talk to when he's ready.

I follow Ted through the house, up the stairs and to the master bedroom. He strips down to his boxer briefs with quick, jerky movements that give away his simmering frustration and slips under the covers without a glance in my direction. I can't deny that it stings.

I remove my own clothes with more care, folding them and setting them out of the way with purposeful movements, willing myself to remain calm. Ted's hurting. It's my job to take care of him right now.

I slide into bed beside him and settle in on my back, staring at the ceiling and denying the impulse to snuggle into him. It's clear that he needs space and, though my injury and the loss of my career can't possibly compare to the loss of a child, I remember being angry with the world once, too. Wanting distance and space and denying myself comfort or sympathy. Even if Ted's loss is decades old, rehashing it with his friends is almost guaranteed to have brought a lot of that pain back to the surface. I'm content to wait him out.

My patience eventually pays off, though I couldn't tell you

how much time has passed when Ted's voice finally startles me out of my thoughts.

"I'm sorry, Zeph."

Frowning, I roll onto my side to face him. The room is dark, lit only by slivers of moonlight filtering in through the curtains, but my eyes adjusted to the darkness a while ago and I can make out the deep furrows in his brow and the tense set of his jaw without issue. "What for?"

I count it as a small victory when he turns his head to face me. "For being an ass tonight. I'm pissed with the situation, not with you."

"I know," I assure him, finally closing the gap between us. I slot myself against his side, nuzzling his jaw. "I get that you're strong, Ted, and that you've been dealing with your grief and loss on your own for almost as long as I've been alive, but I'm here, okay? I'm not forcing you to talk about it," I add quickly when I feel his muscles tighten, "but I'm here."

It takes him a few moments to loosen up again, and his voice is strained and gruff when he says, "Thank you."

This time, the silence between us isn't as loaded, and I shut my eyes and allow the steady rhythm of his heart beating beneath my ear to lull me to sleep.

* * *

I wake up to a cold bed, Ted's spot long empty. He's got a home gym set up in his oversized garage, and I know without having to go searching that that is where I'll find him. We have that in common: the need for physical activity to distract ourselves from our thoughts when things are too overwhelming. I prefer to dance or to run (neither of which activity my knee will thank me for if I go too hard on it) but Ted will hit the rowing machine or attack the weights with gusto. He's even got a punching bag down there, which will also aid him to vent some of his lingering frustration.

Sure enough, when I've made my way down the stairs and back through the too-big space of his home, he's landing blow after blow on the vinyl covered surface, the heavy bag swaying with the force of each hit.

I lean against his car as I watch him, enjoying the ripple of muscle and the droplets of sweat that snake their way down his shirtless form. He's in impeccable shape for a man his age; not bulky but beautifully toned, his skin still mostly elastic and smooth, if a little weathered by time.

Ted completes his last set of swift alternating punches and breathes heavily as he holds the bag to still its movements.

"Enjoying the show?" he asks me with a hint of playfulness, wiping his dripping forehead on his forearm.

I wink at him. "You know it." I cock my head. "You done, or are you going to cool down on the bike?"

It should be strange that I know so much of his exercise routine, but we've worked out here together a few times now. He probably knows mine just as well.

"I'll skip the bike today."

Ignoring the elephant in the room is making me feel antsy, but I promised him that I wouldn't push, so I nod and wrinkle my nose when he steps towards me to press our lips together. "You need a shower," I tell him with a giggle, squirming to avoid having the fresh t-shirt I only slipped on minutes ago wind up victim to the results of his vigorous exercise.

Ted grins and lunges for me, wrapping me in his arms and smothering me while I protest loudly, the effect of my complaints ruined by my ongoing giggles.

"Oh no," he laments dramatically, smirking, "looks like you'll have to shower with me."

"I should punish you," I snark back, "and shower in the guest bathroom just to spite you."

"Now, darling, would you really do that to me?"

I laugh and shake my head at the ridiculous pout that accompanies his question. "No," I answer on a sigh. "That would be as much a punishment to me as it is to you."

"And not of the fun variety."

"Nope."

I feel a flush of relief swoop over and through me at our easy banter now – such a far cry from the tension of last night that I might almost believe I imagined it all.

Until we're back in the bedroom, pulling off our few items of clothing, and Ted suddenly tenses again. "I really am sorry," he says, down to only his underwear and looking more lost and uncertain than I've ever seen him.

"Ted..." I step towards him, reaching out, wanting nothing more than to comfort and assure him that he has *nothing* to apologize for. But he steps back, averting his gaze, as though he's determined to keep punishing himself.

A bizarre thought stirs inside my head at that. Initially, I scoff at myself, thinking it ridiculous. But, as I continue to stand there, my arm outstretched, wanting desperately to do something, literally anything, to help him, it refuses to leave me alone.

Would it even help?

He's my Daddy. I'm his boy. What I'm considering right now completely turns that dynamic on its head.

Just put it out there. You thought it yourself: he's punishing himself. Wipe the slate clean.

Before I can think better of it, I'm clearing my throat and channeling my most authoritative teacher voice, the one I use with the rowdiest of my pre-teen students. "Theodore."

That gets his attention. His head snaps up, his expression startled. "Zephyr, what—?"

"This stops now," I tell him, still firm, no hint of the boy he's used to. I stride over to the bed and sit on the edge, keeping my gaze locked on his. "Over my lap," I demand. "Now."

He balks. "*What?*"

"You seem determined to castigate yourself," I explain, feeling more comfortable with my decision as the realization dawns in his eyes and his shoulders seem to droop, "with no end in sight. We're taking care of that here and now." I pat my thigh, covered only by my tight cotton boxer briefs. "Pants down, over my lap. Now."

His eyes are wide, but he barely hesitates before he complies, dropping his underwear and draping himself over my legs just as instructed. "Good," I praise, stopping shy of completing the phrase. *Good boy* doesn't feel right. Not given our relationship. "Well done," I add instead.

He doesn't reply, but he nods jerkily.

There's obvious tension in his back and shoulders, and I smooth my hand over the expanse of skin, trying to relax him as best I can. "You can safe word at any time," I tell him softly, "but I want you to understand that after I do this…" I pause and remind myself to be assertive and confident in what I'm doing. I can't be hesitant about it, not if I want him to take me seriously. "After I spank you, that's it. You're absolved of whatever it is you're beating yourself up about."

"It's not that simple," he finally argues, and it earns him a swift, stinging slap to one perfect, pale ass cheek. He yelps.

"I want you to imagine this as your absolution," I reiterate firmly. "Compartmentalize everything you're feeling guilty about and let go as I spank you, Ted. Am I understood?"

"Zeph…"

"*Ted.*"

It takes a moment, but he exhales slowly and then nods. "I'll try."

"That's all I ask."

Chapter Fifteen – Ted

If someone had told me even an hour ago that I'd be bent over my boy's lap for a spanking, I'd probably have laughed my ass off at them. But here I am: body tense with anticipation, expecting the first blow.

Honestly, I'm not sure how this is all going to pan out. But I trust Zephyr. Hell, at this point I might even love him. And he's right; I've been beating myself up about everything. Losing Aiden, not being there for him enough in the weeks preceding the accident, keeping the whole story to myself from my friends and every adult relationship I've had…

Well, despite therapy and support groups, it turns out I've still got some deep-seated issues about it all. Who knew?

I knew.

Of course I knew.

All these years, pretending I was fine, keeping it all bottled up… Charlie's concern was probably right on the money, to be honest.

I'm so lost in these thoughts, circling and spiraling in my

head, that the first smack seems to come out of nowhere. The sound of Zephyr's palm meeting the flesh of my ass cheek rings out like an echoing *crack* in the silence of my bedroom and I yelp.

"Easy," he murmurs, rubbing the stinging spot in a gentle caress, "you took that well, Ted."

Some part of me wants to snort with amusement, glad that he's calling me by my name and not Daddy, but what actually bubbles out of me is closer to a sob.

But I don't have time to worry about how much closer I am to breaking point than I thought because Zephyr lands another stinging slap to my ass, on the other cheek this time. It forces a whoosh of breath from my lungs, but he follows it up with another smack, then another, raining them down in rapid succession until I lose count and bow my head.

I'm hardly aware of it happening, but as Zephyr doles out my spanking with confidence, my shoulders loosen and I become boneless against him. I can hear him muttering encouragement, assuring me that I'm doing so well to take the act of domestic discipline as I am, and I'm almost startled to realize that I'm crying when I register the wetness on my cheeks.

It doesn't slow him down, though. He continues on with quick, light smacks that sting almost as much as the initial harder blows did, possibly because the skin is red and sensitive to touch now.

"Come on, Ted, let it all out," his voice is warm and under-standing, and that pushes me over the edge.

I bawl in a way I can't ever recall doing before (not even when I lost Aiden, or when my parents ignored their grandson's death) and, losing all sense of time passing, I accept his continued slaps as my sentence for everything I've been holding in.

And then, without warning, I'm fucking floating.

I'm hardly aware of Zephyr stopping, of him pulling me up into a hug or murmuring those same sweet words of support and encouragement into my ear. I feel high. Cocooned in a bubble of surprising bliss and relaxation.

Subspace.

The word makes its way through the haze in my brain, sobering me a little. Not enough for me to crash yet, but enough for me to understand what it is I'm feeling.

It's completely unexpected.

The extent of my kink and of my exploration into BDSM is literally limited to Daddy/boy play, with experimentation with impact play purely from a Daddy perspective. I've never even thought I personally could, or would, feel this way from being on the receiving end of a spanking.

From what I understood, there are levels of endorphin release required before a sub hits subspace. Zephyr can't have been spanking me for long enough to achieve that, could he?

Or maybe he was. I wasn't exactly paying all that much attention. I was atoning for my perceived sins, after all. Losing myself in the pain and the absolution he offered me.

As I start to come back down, I realize what comes after subspace and the thought is even more sobering: sub-drop.

I've never experienced it, but I've seen it in action. I know everyone is different, too, so there's no way to know how —or even if— it will affect me. I probably need to brace myself for the depression or the irritability, the anxiety and the fatigue that are most commonly associated with the phenomenon, but I haven't the first clue how to do that. It can hit at any time:

moments after the euphoria of subspace fades, or even days.

"Hey, I've got you, Ted."

It's only now that I notice that I'm trembling in Zephyr's embrace. His arms are moving soothingly up and down my back and it is calming me now that I come down from my unexpected high.

"How are you feeling?" he asks, and I can't quite understand where this version of my lover has come from. It should feel strange having the tables turned, having my boy deliver aftercare to me, but it doesn't. "Was that okay?"

This time the snort comes out correctly as a snort and, despite feeling emotionally drained, I have to admit I do feel *lighter* somehow. "It was more than okay, kitten," I tell him, my voice sounding gravelly to my own ears. My throat is tight and scratchy; a sure sign I cried more than I originally thought I did. I try to clear it. "Thank you. I...I needed that." Another incredulous huff escapes me. "How did you know?"

His fingers card through my hair as he answers softly, "I didn't. Not really. I just...*Ugh*. The thought wouldn't go away."

"Hmm, gut instinct, then." I nuzzle into the crook of his neck, feeling vulnerable and almost lost, but also intensely grateful for this beautiful younger man. "Thank you."

Zephyr's quiet for a minute. Contemplative. Then, softly, he asks, "You're still going to be my Daddy, right? This doesn't... uh...it doesn't change everything?"

"Oh, babe, no. It doesn't change a thing."

Although, a little doubt niggles its way into the back of my brain, and I worry that maybe it *does*.

How will he ever look at me the same way again? Even ignoring the past I kept from him, *I'm* supposed to be the authoritative one. The nurturer. What we just did blows all of that to smithereens.

I swallow roughly. "Unless…I mean…" I can't even bring myself to voice those concerns, but he gets it.

"Ted, no. Whatever you're thinking, stop it." Zephyr shakes his head. "I was worried you wouldn't see *me* as your boy anymore," he confesses, as if he's somehow reading my thoughts. "It doesn't change the way I see you at all."

"Really?" I hate that my voice comes out so small and uncertain, seemingly proving to myself that my fears are valid. But Zephyr rolls his eyes and smirks at me, the hint of sassiness easing my mind more than his words can do on their own.

"Really," he insists. "You're still my Daddy, Ted. For as long as you'll have me as your boy. I…" he swallows, "I love you."

If I thought I was on a high during subspace, it's nothing compared to the electric warmth that floods me with his simple declaration. I know it's not just lip service, either. Not with what we've just done today.

Choked up, I respond, "God, Zeph, I love you, too."

Then we're kissing, and we're both crying, but they're happy tears. Tears of relief. Of mutual joy. Of love.

Then his hands slip lower down my back, brushing over the heated skin on my ass and I hiss into his mouth.

He pulls back, startled and chagrined. "Oh, shit, sorry!"

I can't help laughing, feeling lighter than I have in…Christ, lighter than I can *ever* remember feeling. I know that part of that is still the lingering endorphins from the intense scene we just took part in —from reaching fucking subspace— and the other part is the rush of affection from our mutual declarations of love, but for now that's enough.

"It's fine," I tell him, rubbing our noses together. "It's a reminder of how damn much you care about me."

"Still, we should get you some lotion." He crinkles his nose adorably. "And we still need to shower."

The thought of hot water on my stinging backside is not appealing. "Lukewarm water only."

His expression softens out into understanding and fondness. "Yes, Daddy."

As we make our way into the bathroom, I can't help but feel optimistic that, with Zephyr at my side, everything's going to be just fine.

Chapter Sixteen – Zephyr

"Wait…*what*?!" Ash asks me, his jaw dropping now that I've finished giving him the abridged version of what happened over the weekend after Ted and I left his house.

It's Wednesday again, and this time we're having lunch on our own, so we've been free to talk as one Little to another. Ted and I are solid, and we spent most of Sunday reassuring each other that we're still Daddy and boy, that nothing has to change, but I still need to talk this out with someone who will understand my perspective better.

"Uh huh," I answer, shoveling a forkful of lettuce into my mouth. I chew it and swallow as quickly as I possibly can. "I don't know what came over me. But he was *so* in his head and so determined to…to beat himself up and I just…*snapped*, I guess."

"Jesus," my friend sits back in his seat, dumbfounded. "I just can't imagine it."

"Well, I'd rather you didn't," I tease, going in for another mouthful of my salad. He scrunches up a paper napkin and tosses it at me.

"Not what I meant!"

I snicker.

"Seriously," he leans forward across the small café table, lowering his voice, "I couldn't possibly spank Charlie. I mean, he's my Daddy. It would feel weird." He cocks his head. "Did it feel weird?"

"Oddly enough, no." I've been thinking about that more than anything. I sigh. "And *that's* what freaks me out. Like, if the roles we play are Daddy and boy, why didn't it feel weird to dominate Ted? Doesn't that, like, go against the whole dynamic?"

Ash doesn't answer immediately. He takes a sip of his lemonade and seems to give my question some proper thought. "I mean," he starts, tilting his head from side to side as he continues to think out loud, "it doesn't have to be weird. It worked, right? Like, it helped him deal with…uh…everything?" Neither one of us wants to actually talk about Ted's past. It feels wrong, somehow. Disrespectful. I just nod, rolling my wrist in a gesture for him to keep talking. "And you're both adults, so…maybe look at it as you knowing what he needed? Just like he knows what you need when you're little for him."

"But you just said—"

"I know. And, because Charlie and I have never been in that sort of situation, I can only say that it would probably feel weird for us. But," he holds up a finger to stall me from saying anything, his mop of curly hair swaying as he moves, "when I really think about it, it shouldn't feel weird to do something to help him, Daddy or not."

I take a moment to process that, relaxing back into my chair and letting the general din of the café fill the silence between us. It's busy for a Wednesday lunch time, with people chatting at tables around us, the sounds of cutlery hitting plates and the muted clanging of pots and pans from the kitchen reminding me that life goes on despite my personal dramas. It's strangely comforting in its own way.

"You're right," I eventually acknowledge, pushing the remnants of my salad into the middle of the table. "It felt good to step up and do something, you know? And the fact that he trusted me…" Now I choke up a little, recalling how emotional the whole experience was.

Ash reaches across the laminate tabletop and squeezes my hand. "I'm glad you're there for him. Charlie feels awful…"

"I can imagine."

Ted and I haven't spoken about how he's going to handle his next interaction with his friends. It's not my place to push him, after all. Not about that. I wanted him to stop blaming himself. To stop hurting himself. But, beyond that, how he goes forward from here is all on him. I'll support him, but I won't force the issue. Suffice to say, I've learned my lesson about that.

"And I have no idea what to say to him, either," Ash goes on, listlessly dragging a soggy looking fry across his plate. "I mean, poor Ted."

I grimace. "Yeah, look; that's exactly what he's wanted to avoid all these years. Being treated differently once everyone knew about…*y'know.*"

Across from me, Ash drops the fry and frowns. "But we love him. If we'd known—"

"It wouldn't have changed anything." I can say this with finality.

Again, though I know that the end of my dancing career can't possibly compare to the loss of a child, I understand exactly where Ted's coming from when he emphatically states that he doesn't want to be pitied.

"It wouldn't have changed his past," I add. "It wouldn't have changed the years he's spent grieving privately. It wouldn't have changed the man or even the Daddy that he is today. All it would have done is make you all treat him with kid gloves that he really doesn't want you to." I run my hand through my hair as I try to explain, "All he wants is to be treated the same way as always, and he's afraid that's not going to happen. I mean, he's built his whole life up after everything fell apart – he doesn't want that taken from him."

I can tell Ash wants to argue with me, but something I've said must have gotten through to him because all he does is bite his lip and nod. "Yeah, okay. I get that."

If only the others can be convinced.

* * *

The rest of my day after meeting Ash for lunch is uneventful. At least, until I'm locking up the studio for the night.

"Zephyr," I just about jump out of my skin at the sound of London's voice. He and Matt approach from where they must have been waiting for me, leaning against a parked car on the street outside my workplace.

Because this isn't creepy or overstepping at all...

I frown at them both. "Uh, hi?"

They spare me the small talk and get straight to the point. "Ash called," Matt says, rubbing the back of his neck.

Of course he did.

London pulls Matt in against him in a comforting gesture. It's sweet watching them together, these two burly men whose personalities seem at odds with their aesthetic. "We're not, like, trying to get you to take us to Ted or anything."

I smile softly at London's assurances. The weekend was the first time he and I have actually spoken to each other and, after seeing me in my dress, it was surprising when he quietly started up a conversation about the best places to buy panties and other pretty things.

I'm under the impression that none of the others (bar Matt, obviously) know about London's penchant for lace, and I'm honored that he trusted me with his secret. It is that, and that alone, which has me open to hearing them out about Ted, even though I know my Daddy would be uncomfortable with the idea of this conversation taking place.

With a sigh, I adjust the strap of my duffel bag on my shoulder and ask, "So…why are you here, then?"

Matt shifts his weight on his feet awkwardly, like he's not quite sure how to explain himself. "Just…uh…we wanted to let you know that we're not gonna get all weird on him."

I blink.

Really? This is information that couldn't have been sent over text?

As if reading my thoughts, London chuckles and shrugs. "We were heading out for dinner down the block and…well, I guess you can't really get sincerity or tone out of a text message. Matt figured we'd kill two birds with one stone."

"Right." I'm not entirely sure that I believe them, but they mean well nonetheless.

"It's just, y'know, I care about Ted. A lot. I mean, our whole group does." Matt shoves his hands in his pockets. "And, if I know him, he's going to avoid us all like the plague until he's convinced this has blown over. But I thought that he might listen if it came from you." A soft smile plays across his lips as he exchanges a meaningful look with London. "If you're anything like us, anyway." He sighs heavily. "Plus, I get where he's coming from. I mean, it's not the same, but I almost walked away from the guys—"

"*What?*" I can't withhold my startled interruption. A woman walking past our assembled group jumps at my voice and I offer her an apologetic grimace before she walks on.

Matt brushes my concern off with a vague gesture of his hand. "It was ages ago. But I wasn't in the best place emotionally or mentally, and I started shutting everyone out while I tried to avoid their pity. It sucked, man. And I don't like to think of Ted being in the same boat."

Having had similar thoughts myself, I can only nod. "He'll get there," I assure Matt. "He tried really hard over the weekend to work through some of his issues, but he's going to see his therapist again this week because the whole mess has stirred up stuff he thought was buried. Just…give him some time, okay?"

I'm relieved when Matt's expression doesn't fall. He genuinely seems to understand what I'm saying and isn't going to push the issue. I shouldn't be surprised, really. I knew that Ted's friends are good guys. But seeing it in action still gives me a minor jolt of convoluted emotions anyway.

Would things have been different if I'd had a support network like these guys?

I try to brush the thought away. I've moved on. Besides, through Ted, I have these guys myself now. The fact that they've sought me out and have taken me into their confidence is proof of that.

I wonder if I've given some of my thoughts away again somehow, because London claps a hand on my shoulder and squeezes, saying, "You know if you need to talk, we're here for you, too, okay?"

"Thanks," I reply, then start moving towards my car, parked a few doors up the street from the studio. "I appreciate that." I grin at them and wave them on, effectively ending the conversation. "Enjoy your dinner!"

During the short drive back to my apartment, I consider Matt's words and hope that Ted trusts his friends enough to reach out to them, too. They are good people, all of them, and Ted needs more than what I alone can offer him, even if we both wished otherwise.

Chapter Seventeen – Ted

It takes two weeks (inclusive of three sessions with my therapist) before I feel confident and comfortable to turn the notifications in the group chat back on.

Zephyr told me that the guys have been reaching out to him, asking about me, and I know I can't avoid them forever. Hell, they've given me more space and time than I've ever given them, and I'm grateful for that. But now it's time to ease back into my friendships and accept their support.

I lock myself in my office and spend my Friday morning scrolling through the thread, snorting at some of the banter between my friends.

Josh, naturally, posts inappropriate and outlandish memes and deliberately stirs the others up. The fact that Charlie takes the bait every single time is more amusing than it has any right to be and reading the way the rest of the group take turns escalating the situation has my chest tight with a mixture of emotions. Regret. Fondness. Nostalgia. Hope. They all twist together while I read the latest ridiculous interaction as it plays out in real time.

Josh: I've decided I need a harem of men.

Charlie: ...a harem?

Spencer: Don't knock it, C-man. There's a whole romance sub-genre for that kind of thing.

Chance: Read any good ones lately?

Spencer: So... @Josh, a harem?

Josh: Yeah. I'm thinking a mechanic, a hairdresser, a super hot investor, a doctor, a tattoo artist and a masseur.

Josh: It's almost like a Julie Andrews song if you pace it out right.

Ash: Boy, 'The Sound of Music' sure has changed since I last watched it.

Charlie: Baby, don't encourage him.

Spencer: These ARE a few of my favorite things...

Josh: And somehow my version is still less gay than the musical.

Charlie sends a GIF of Captain Picard facepalming.

I chuckle out loud, startling myself with the sound. And how sad is that? That I've been in such a dark place that the sound of my own laughter is foreign to my own ears... A wave of melancholy threatens to overwhelm me and I sigh.

Zephyr's been supportive, and I know he's been keeping the group posted about me, but I really do miss my friends. I miss the laughter and the ridiculous shit we talk about. I'm not in my early twenties anymore: I have a network of people who genuinely give a crap about me, and being alone just because I want to avoid the sympathy and the hard conversations is somehow more difficult now than it was in the months after the accident.

I turn my attention back to the group chat which is picking up pace again.

London: I legit ignored my phone for 10 mins & I missed the entire harem convo. Devastated.

Matt: Excuse you, but why do you need a harem anyway???

London: Like you weren't imagining your own dream team.

Chance: Come on, guys, break it up. Flirt it up in a private thread.

Chance: And don't think I didn't see you avoiding my question earlier @Spencer.

Chance follows up his second message with an 'I'm watching you' GIF of some woman gesturing at her eyes with two fingers and then pointing them at the viewer.

Spencer: No hablo ingles.

He completes the sentiment with a shrugging emoji.

Spencer: @Josh, you didn't explain what brought the whole harem idea on, anyway.

Josh: I'm checking out Grindr. So many choices, so not enough time.

Charlie: Gentlemen, I give you our city's tax dollars hard at work protecting our community. & LOL @Spencer. Smooth, my friend. Real smooth.

Josh: Fuck you, Charlie, I'm on my lunch break.

Josh adds a middle finger emoji. Spencer interjects with a GIF of a dog wearing sunglasses.

I shake my head, my spirits buoyed by the ridiculous conversation. It's good to know that they're all the same, that the world has kept turning in the two weeks I've spent feeling out of sorts. It's also a sign that I might just be able to drop back into the fold without too much drama.

God only knows the way I overreacted and overthought things was dramatic enough. I'm embarrassed by that more than I can properly explain, which also hasn't helped with my intentions to ease back into my social circle.

Before I know it, my fingers are tapping out a comment of my own and I'm pressing the little 'send' button.

Ted: I didn't realize the pickings at The Grove had gotten so slim that you needed to turn to Grindr to hook up.

It's clunky as far as playful ribbing goes, but I hope it shows them that I'm trying and that nothing has to change.

There's what equates to a stunned silence in the thread before the notifications that people are typing pop up. I watch the screen with bated breath.

Josh's reply hits first.

Josh: Ted, man, I tell you...there's a drought of Daddies right now and it sucks. A series of emojis follow the words. The crying face a few times, the poop emoji, and the angry face.

Josh: If you didn't have Z, I'd tell you to get your ass down there and have your choice of Littles.

I glance at the clock and gauge that Zephyr is probably in the middle of teaching a hip hop class right now. I can only imagine what his reaction to that last message will be. I kind of want to see it. I like it when he gets sassy and territorial. It's hot.

Chance's is the next message to pop up, distracting me from those thoughts.

Chance: @Ted You're honestly surprised by anything Josh says these days, dude? Also @Josh maybe that's a sign you've gone through too many Daddies. Chased 'em all off.

Spencer follows almost immediately after.

Spencer: Kid's probably scared all the Daddies away with his bratty-ass ways.

Spencer: @Chance Damn it! You beat me to it!

Chance: Not my fault I'm quicker at typing.

While the note appears to say that Spencer is composing his

reply, Ash's name appears on my screen.

Ash: Welcome back, Uncle Ted. I've missed you.

Before I can reply, he posts again.

Ash: Especially 'cos nobody else can keep this bunch in line as well as you.

Charlie: Hey! What am I, chopped liver?

Ash: Sorry, but you know it's the truth, Daddy. He sends a GIF of a teddy bear blowing a kiss, either to tease his husband or soften the blow of his words. Potentially both.

My lips pull into a grin and, before I can stop myself, I'm typing again.

Ted: Brains over brawn, Charlie.

Charlie sends back a line of middle finger emojis and I crack up, more of the tension in my shoulders and chest easing. It looks like things don't have to change after all, and I'm ashamed that I underestimated my friends so badly.

As I said before, my own reaction to having my past exposed surprised and embarrassed me. I'm the oldest of our group, and I suppose I had always thought of myself as the most stable. But panicking over the idea that they'd treat me differently says otherwise, doesn't it?

My therapist, Sandra, suggested that it's likely I haven't worked through my hang-ups about being a grieving father who turned to Daddy play as a means of escapism. That I'm still stuck on my fears that the guys might think it weird or perverted or God only knows what.

And she's probably right.

The fact that it took my boy spanking some sense into me to clear my head enough to seek help is another giveaway. On some level, I'm still feeling guilty and still feel like I'm doing something wrong, something deserving of punishment and scorn.

Sandra also suspects that I'm also more likely to be feeling raw, given that what would have been Aiden's thirtieth birthday is looming only a couple of months away now.

"There are words for spouses who lose their husbands or wives, and for children who lose their parents, but no word to describe a parent whose child has died," she said in our first session and those words come back to me now. "Because it's unthinkable, Ted. And it's understandable to continue to grieve and feel that pain, even twenty-eight years after the fact. Letting others see that you're struggling with it, especially around milestone dates, doesn't have to be a bad thing. You don't have to be strong and rational all the time. You're human."

The thing is, I know these things. I know that if my position was reversed and it was one of the other guys struggling, I'd tell him all the same stuff Sandra has said to me. But my main issue is pride and I know it. And I'm slowly working through it. The fact that the guys are letting me slip back into the chat without a fuss makes it easier.

Speaking of...

My phone's ringing brings me out of my thoughts and I'm not surprised to see Charlie's name (accompanied by a photo of him goofing around as he dressed for his wedding) flash on my screen.

What does surprise me is my lack of any inner-turmoil as I answer.

"Hi Charlie."

"Hey," he greets me, then pauses awkwardly. I hate that my issues have played such a large role in putting this distance between us. He clears his throat. "Brains over brawn, huh?"

I chuckle at his attempt to break the ice and lean back in my office chair, refraining from propping my feet up on my desk, though the urge to stretch out is there. "You always take the bait so well."

"Heh," he offers his own huff of amusement and I can imagine him blushing a little, "I guess I do." There's another pause before he says, "I, uh, I wanted to apologize properly, Ted."

"I appreciate that," I respond easily, having anticipated something like this from him. I've even spoken to Sandra about it. "But you don't really have anything to apologize for. Not really."

"I was kind of a dick, man. I mean, before everything went down. I…" he clears his throat, "I told myself I was giving you the space you asked for but, honestly? I was being selfish because I had no idea what to say to you. And that was wrong of me. And then I wouldn't let it go, and everything went to hell, and—"

"Charlie, it's fine. Really."

This time it genuinely is. I admit that I was annoyed with him at first. Irritated that he had made such a big deal out of his sister's throwaway words, to the point where I'd felt backed into a corner. But distance, therapy, and time to think have helped me work through those frustrations, too. And, honestly, I can't hold it against my best friend that he was being hypersensitive on my behalf, can I? Not when I miss his company as badly as I do. He meant well. He cared. That means something to me, even if the way he showed it was frustrating.

"I'm still—"

"I swear, if you apologize again, I'm going to put you in a corner for ten minutes the next time I see you."

As expected, my threat earns me a laugh. "I'd like to see you try, old man," he taunts. "I'm not the Walker who responds to those sorts of consequences."

"Like your bratty brother really does, either." Not that I can say I've tried to school Josh. A Little though he might be, he's also not my type. He's also beyond the age limit I'm comfortable pursuing…but that's irrelevant because I'm a taken man anyway. Well, I am now. And I wouldn't trade Zephyr for anything.

"You'd still have more luck disciplining him than a fellow Daddy and you know it." Charlie's response cuts off the strange path my thoughts just went down. "But I was actually talking about Ash."

"Either way," I acknowledge, "I'm happy to leave Josh to another unsuspecting Daddy."

Charlie chuckles and, after a few more lighthearted exchanges, reluctantly says, "Alright, I'd better run, but…Ted?"

"Hmm?"

"It's good to hear your voice. I've missed you."

I nod, despite knowing that he can't see me. "I've missed you, too, bud."

After we hang up, my phone pings again, but it's a text message from Zephyr. My heart squeezes as I read it.

'Taking a 5 min break. Saw that you're back in the group chat. I'm proud of you, Daddy.'

'Are we still on for tonight?' I text him back, already thinking of all the ways I'm going to show him my appreciation for not running away at the first sign of my meltdown. I know I wouldn't have gotten through any of this if not for him.

'Sure are. I'm breaking in that pretty yellow dress you bought me.'

I grin, already imagining him wearing it and tap out my

response, *'I can't wait, kitten.'*

* * *

"Another tea, Daddy?"

As promised, Zephyr and I are back in our usual routine. I helped him change into his new yellow sundress, delighting in how well the bright color suits him, and then settled in for a tea party. Even though I was a little concerned that our dynamic might be strange after he spanked me, it doesn't feel like anything between us has changed.

He's still my princess, still comfortable to indulge in his kink around me, and still happy to call me Daddy and allow me to join in his play.

The relief I feel at that is palpable.

"Yes please," I lift my delicate cup up for him to pour a measure of water for me from the functional teapot I bought when Ash first started coming around regularly. The dolls and teddy bears on either side of me aren't as lucky: their cups are full of air alone.

He chatters away as he's prone to do when he's being the host of such a gathering, and I'm once again struck dumb by how beautiful he is. I know that I've told him that I love him but, in moments like these, I don't think the words properly capture how he makes me feel.

It's like he was made for me. There's no push and pull with him, just an effortless flow to our time together. He's not demanding or needy even though he jokes that he is, and he knows exactly what to say or do even at times where I have no idea what I need from him.

I know he's put two and two together and worked out why

I keep our sexual relationship separate from our Daddy/boy relationship, but he's been good about not pushing me to talk about it. Even before he learned about my past and about Aiden, he didn't demand any further information from me after I safe worded. He understood that I was uncomfortable and left it at that.

He's perfect. Utterly, completely perfect, and he's rapidly becoming the center of my universe.

"Dance with me, Daddy?"

The question takes me off guard, interrupting my saccharine thoughts and I blink at him. "What, baby?"

Zephyr pushes to his feet and extends his hand to me. "Dance with me? Like we're at a ball?"

In all the time that we've spent together, he's never made this suggestion before. I'm not sure what to expect. Does Little Zephyr dance fluidly, with grace and poise and the professionalism that comes from years of training? Or does Little Zephyr step on his Daddy's toes and stomp around a makeshift or imaginary dance floor with the enthusiasm, lack of coordination, and the blissful ignorance of youth?

Honestly, I don't know which I'd prefer. I feel like the latter option would be adorable, but the former would be beautiful. Either way, I know this is something that means a lot to him. More than the too-casual request would have me believing, in fact.

"I'd love to." I take his hand and smother a groan as he helps me back up into a standing position.

I might be healthy and fit for my age, but I'm still forty-seven. I'm just not built for sitting cross-legged on the floor for extended periods of time anymore.

Zephyr smiles a bright, childish smile at me before he prances over to the Bluetooth speaker on the bookshelf, turning it on and then reaching for his phone, fiddling until the 'boop' of a successful connection sounds out from the speaker.

Then he presses play on one of his many playlists and the sound of classical, orchestral music fills the air, violins at the fore.

"Strauss," I recognize instantly, because even someone with zero classical training knows *The Blue Danube*.

My boy's expression turns indulgent. "Clever," he says, then grabs my hand and tugs me into the open space beside the bed, away from the tea party set up on the floor. There's not a huge amount of floor space here, but we'll manage.

Manhandling me until my hands are positioned the way he wants them, Zephyr steps in close, pressing against me as he leads us in a limited waltz to the music. I'm not at all disappointed to find that he's dancing gracefully and not clumsily like one might expect from a child. This is ingrained into him, after all. And he began learning ballroom dance at an early age besides.

Step back, step to the side, slide feet together. Step back, step to the side, slide feet together. The motion is easy to follow, aided by the music. We glide across the carpet in our contained square of space, and after a little while, Zephyr rests his head on my shoulder and turns us around, changing his movement, allowing me to suddenly lead the dance. *Forward, side, come together. Forward, side, come together.*

"You're good at this, Daddy," he murmurs against my chest.

I smile and kiss the top of his head. "It's not my first dance, darling…but I am a bit rusty."

His giggle is light and tinkling. "I wasn't gonna say anything."

I lower the hand on his waist and pinch his ass, making him

squeal. "Cheeky."

We waltz together for a little while longer, until the song fades out and a new one begins. Zephyr pulls away and curtsies, pulling the hem of his skirt out widely on either side of him. "Thank you for the dance, good sir."

Chuckling, I bow. "And thank you, tiny dancer."

He claps his hands together. "Okay, tidy up time!"

I love that he still follows the rules and routine that we discussed that very first night together. In hindsight, I can't believe that I suspected he'd be bratty and naughty. Yes, he's sassy and cheeky, but my boy has a praise kink a mile wide: being a good boy is far more enjoyable for him.

Together we pack up the dolls, teddies and the tea set, setting aside the two cups we drank from, as well as the teapot itself, to be washed downstairs. Then, once the space is orderly again, Zephyr tugs his dress over his head. He carefully puts it on a hanger and ducks into the walk-in robe to hang it with care. This leaves him in the lacy white thong he arrived in (which he'd been wearing beneath his jeans until playtime: a very welcome surprise for me) and nothing else.

I swallow reflexively as he saunters back out of the walk-in, swinging his hips and stalking towards me like I'm his prey.

"We should go dancing for real sometime," he tells me, his dark eyes smoldering, no hint of his Little persona to be found.

At this point, I'd agree to almost anything he says. "Sounds good," I tell him, my voice having taken on a husky bite.

Zephyr's lips quirk upwards, like he knows exactly what he's doing to me. And, hell, he probably does.

Chapter Eighteen – Zephyr

Ted laughs as we tumble into his bed, and the sound is music to my ears. I haven't seen or heard him feel so free in weeks. I'm not deluded enough to think that his issues have all been resolved, because mental health does *not* work that way, but between talking things out at his own pace and seeing his therapist, he seems genuinely happier again. Closer to the man I met at Asher's wedding.

I can't properly express just how excited I was to see that he had commented playfully in the group chat earlier today. If nothing else, that was the biggest sign that he's starting to heal again. And I was immensely grateful to the rest of the guys for playing it cool and treating him the same way they always have. Even though both Matt and Ash told me they would, seeing it in action was far more reassuring.

"You're thinking too hard," Ted complains lightly, nipping at my bottom lip, "which means I'm not doing my job right."

"Speaking of too hard…" Snickering, I arch my body into his, rubbing our lengths together. He's still way overdressed in comparison to me, seeing as I'm only wearing a lacy thong and he's in his jeans. We discarded his shirt somewhere on the way to the bedroom.

Ted groans against my mouth. "God, I feel like a fucking teenager when I'm with you."

"I mean, I'm in my thirties, so *that's* disturbing."

"Brat."

"You love it."

His gaze softens and he ghosts his lips over mine, whispering, "I love *you*."

Every time he says those words, I feel like I could just float away. "I love you, too."

When we kiss again, it's slow and sweet. Our tongues intertwine almost lazily while Ted's hands traverse my body, igniting fire beneath my skin. Our hips rock together and I sigh into his mouth.

"Your jeans have to come off," I tell him, keeping my voice low and gentle, not wanting to break the mood.

"Mmm," he agrees, but makes no move to put the acknowledgment into action.

I giggle and attempt to undo his fly, distracted by the way he's now nuzzling at the crook of my neck, licking and sucking the path his hands only just traveled.

"Oh, fuck, Ted," I gasp when he gets to my nipple, arching my back when he rolls the little nub of flesh between his teeth. It's almost like there's a direct line between my nipples and my cock, because jolts of pleasure seem to shoot straight down to my already hard and aching length. "Yes," I breathe, the 's' sibilant as I draw the word out, "more."

He shuffles us around until I'm flat on my back and he's replaced his teeth with his thumb and index finger, moving his mouth to my other nipple.

"Jesus…fuck…" It's like my pleasure receptors have all lit up, synapses firing through all my nerve endings.

His resulting chuckle is deep and rich. I think I'd like to record the sound and keep it on repeat. Maybe make it my ringtone or text alert tone or something.

"Pants," I remind him before I lose all control of my thoughts. "Pants off now. *Please.*" I bite back the instinct to add 'Daddy' to my plaintive whine.

I haven't called him Daddy in bed since before everything went down at Ash and Charlie's place. While he didn't seem to have an issue with it before, I'm not sure I'm comfortable pushing that boundary right now. And I really don't want to stop what we're doing to have a heart-to-heart about it. That can happen later.

Thankfully, Ted takes pity on me and pulls away to struggle out of his jeans and boxer briefs. I lick my lips as his beautiful cock springs free of its confines, hard and glistening invitingly at the tip. But, before I can beg him to fuck my face, he's crawled back over to me and has hooked his fingers into the delicate band of my thong.

Ted is ever so gentle as he eases the material over the slight curve of my hips and down my long legs, careful not to stretch or tear the lace. He tosses it over his shoulder once it's free of my ankles and licks a stripe over my balls and shaft, making me whimper.

But instead of sucking me down, he settles his body over mine, sliding our cocks together. I moan at the feeling of skin meeting skin, the glide aided by our combined pre-cum. It gets even better when Ted adds lube to the equation, but he doesn't jerk us off together. He just slicks us both up, then settles back over me again, bracing his forearms on either side of my head before he starts rocking his hips in earnest.

I can't remember the last time I got off like this with another man. Blow jobs and hand jobs and occasional anal, sure, but frottage? As my eyes roll back in my head, I question why I haven't done this more often.

"You feel amazing, kitten," Ted murmurs, nibbling at my earlobe while he continues to drag his cock alongside mine. His hips are pressed close to mine, the friction and pressure of his body providing the perfect amount of stimulation right where I need it most. With every thrust, the pleasure mounts.

"Oh...*God*..." I can feel my brain turning to mush as the sensation escalates. He starts to swivel his hips a little and I can feel my cock dripping as I get closer to the edge, a ball of delicious tension tightening somewhere in my gut as my balls draw upwards.

Ted keeps talking, his voice husky as he whispers, "You..." he exhales roughly, "you fit against me so perfectly, Zeph..."

I wonder if he can feel just how rapidly my heart is beating. Even though we've made love slowly before, this feels different somehow. More intense, even though he's not even inside me.

I have the strangest urge to hold him tight, tears —of love, of happiness, of empathy for the pain of his past— burning my eyes and threatening to spill down my cheeks. I want to meld into him, to somehow extend this experience forever.

"Feels...so...good." These words that I offer him in return are nowhere near enough to properly express any of what I'm feeling, but they'll have to do, even if my voice is curiously tight even to my own ears.

Ted's mouth descends over mine again in yet another gentle kiss and now my tears do spill over, because I'm convinced that I can feel all the same things in this kiss that I couldn't quite put into words. I close my eyes as they trickle out of the corners and down the sides of my face.

He shifts his weight so he can bring one of his hands up to cup my cheek, smoothing his thumb over the tracks my tears are making. "Baby…"

"I'm good," I assure him, forcing my eyes back open. My smile feels tremulous, but it's genuine. "I just…this is…" I gasp on another thrust, the movement causing his belly to brush over my sensitive cock head, "I love you."

Dipping his head down, he brings our lips back together and this time the kiss is harder and more desperate. As though we've given ourselves a green light, our hips pick up pace and our breathing intensifies.

Ted pulls away from the kiss and rests his forehead on mine. "Oh, fuck, Zeph, I'm gonna…" his deep warning is cut off by his blissed-out groan and I feel his cock pulse next to mine, then the heat and wetness of his release between our bodies.

With his cum coating my cock, I cry out after a few more shaky thrusts, adding my own mess to his.

"Wow…" I utter, catching my breath in the afterglow. "That was…" Intense. Emotional. Beautiful. Special. Unexpected. None of the words that spring to mind completely cover the way I'm feeling.

Ted's fingers card through my hair. "Yeah," he agrees quietly, even though I haven't finished my assessment out loud. "It was."

I snuggle into his side, heedless of the discomfort of our fluids drying on my skin. There's time for a shower or a bath later. Right now, I want to soak in how right this moment feels. How right it feels to be held in his arms right here in his home:

the same place that so intimidated me the first time I visited.

I relish in the comfort I feel here now. I'm able to see this place, Ted's home, the way I should have to begin with. It's grand, yes, but it's also an extension of him. His warmth and vibrancy are imbued in it.

It's in the artwork he chose for the walls. It's in the few photographs on the mantle over the fireplace, including one of Aiden, which I watched him place there with shaking hands just last week. It's in the meticulously planned details of his renovations, and in the careful drape of his jacket over the back of the chair by the bay window on the other sided of this very bedroom. The whole place *screams* 'Ted', and I can't imagine him living anywhere else now.

In addition to that, I soak in the feelings of utter relief washing over me.

The relief of our relationship seeming stronger than ever, of Ted working towards a healthier way of living with his grief and trauma, and of knowing that he's ready to let me and the guys in. It all settles in my bones, filling me with warmth and contentment.

From my own experience, I know that it's going to be a roller-coaster from here. Ted's bound to have downs as well as ups. I mean, I still do and I always will. But, together with the tight knit circle of friends he and Ash have introduced me to, we're going to support each other at our own pace, and it's going to be okay.

Epilogue – Ted

"Are you sure you want me to come with you?" Zephyr chews his bottom lip, his dark eyes searching mine from the passenger seat of my car. "I can wait here if you're more comfortable with that."

I reach across the center console and squeeze his hand. I appreciate that he's so concerned for me. God only knows that I've given him and the guys plenty of reasons to feel that way over the last few months. Nevertheless, I'm confident in my decision today. "I want you with me," I tell him firmly. "I *need* you with me."

Six months ago, I would have been too proud to admit that. I was, as Ash likes to tease me, the Daddy of our whole group. Daddy of Daddies. Strong. Stalwart. Stable. I wasn't supposed to show weakness or need help. Yeah, I'm aware of the hypocrisy there, the advice I've given Charlie (or, to a lesser degree, Spence and Chance) over the years somehow never applicable to me personally.

But now? With therapy and multiple deep and meaningful

discussions with my friends (which turned out to be far easier to face than I'd imagined they would be), I can admit when I'm struggling.

I still find it difficult to do; don't get me wrong. But I *can* do it, and the end result of asking for help is usually worth having to bite back my pride and ignore my hang-ups.

Case in point: Zephyr offers me a smile full of empathy and understanding as he nods and opens his car door. I meet him on the grassy verge next to the curb where I parked, and he holds out his hand for me to take. My grip tightens almost imperceptibly as we walk across the immaculate lawn to our destination.

It's been years since I've been here. Too long, really.

In my other hand, I clutch a small bouquet of flowers and my chest aches when I finally place them down on the smooth marble headstone engraved with my son's name and dates of birth and death.

In my head, I make my apologies: for never visiting his resting place, for having missed his thirtieth birthday, for essentially having kept him a secret for my entire adult life. But I don't say anything aloud. Big, impassioned speeches to invisible audiences have never really been my style, and I'm not deluded enough to think that, even if he could hear me, this would be my only chance to tell him any of this.

Zephyr doesn't push me, either. He just holds my hand and lets me breathe and think whatever I need to.

Some part of me was afraid that I wouldn't be able to handle this moment. That facing Aiden's headstone would trigger another meltdown or something similar. But, though I feel the pang of loss again, and my chest aches, I don't feel any worse for having finally visited for the first time in years.

If anything, guilt begins to lift from my shoulders.

When all is said and done, this is just another location. Visiting (or not visiting) doesn't change my past or absolve me of my perceived sins or shortcomings. The only person judging me for how and when I choose to remember my son is me, and I've been too hard on myself for too long.

It's funny that doing the one thing I told myself I never would turned out to be the thing I needed to do in order to truly start to process and heal. Well, as much as anyone who has lost a loved one can.

(I still refuse to tell Charlie he was right, even if we both know that he was.)

"Thank you for coming with me," I say later, when Zephyr and I are on the drive back to our hotel. It's the first I've spoken since we approached Aiden's grave, and I'm beyond grateful that Zephyr understood what I needed.

He always seems to just know.

In fact, the evening proves to be another example of just that. When we're safely ensconced in the lavish suite I insisted on paying for, Zephyr sits on the edge of the bed and pats his lap.

"I think you need this," he says softly when my heart leaps into my throat and tears of gratitude prick at my eyes.

I swallow roughly and nod.

Neither one of us question how or why this works for us anymore. Perhaps it's something I've always needed and never knew it? Or maybe it's just Zephyr's attention and love that makes it feel so right. Either way, I trust him in a way I've never trusted anyone, and it allows me to let go completely.

In turn, the next night we're back to being Daddy and Little Zeph, and I watch how free he is with me.

I marvel over how much he has grown as a person since

we met, too. He was anxious when I first met him, though he had been doing his best to hide it. He'd been learning to re-embrace his kinks and his identity in Little space, and his bravery to try it all with a complete stranger —*with me*— was astounding even then. Now he is brazen and dominating when he's big, and bright, bubbly and confident when he's little. It's an intoxicating mix, but not one I'd ever have labeled my 'type' before now.

Honestly, Zephyr is everything I never knew I needed.

"Whatcha thinking about, Daddy?" he asks, having just spent the last ten minutes dancing across the large, open space of the hotel room. His cheeks are flushed, and his eyes are shining, and I am struck yet again by how insanely beautiful he is.

I stand up from my seat in the 'audience' (on the bed) and walk towards him. He squeaks when I pull him in for a hug.

"Just thinking about how lucky I am to have found you when I did, tiny dancer."

"Hmm," he murmurs against my chest, sounding less child-like now as he comes back out of his little head space. "I'm lucky too."

I pull backwards and tilt his head up to meet mine, bringing our lips together in a gentle kiss that says more than I can properly put into words. I love him. I'm grateful for him. I'm amazed by him. I trust him.

I need him.

Even though the kiss was sweet, we're both breathing heavily as we part. "Zeph," I whisper his name into the small pocket of air between us, my voice thin with a desperation that seems to have sneaked up on me, "Baby, I want you to fuck me."

We talked about it once months ago, and then in the ensuing drama of my meltdown, we never brought it up again. It wasn't until this moment that I realized how badly I want to do this: to share something with him that I've never had with anyone else. It seems only fitting that we do this here, on neutral ground, taking advantage of a moment already so fully imbued with emotion.

He inhales sharply and his dark eyes are intense and focused as he looks into mine. Little Zephyr is gone and he's most certainly back in his adult head space. "Are you sure?"

I cup his clean shaven jaw with my palm, smoothing my thumb over the subtle prickle of today's growth as I nod. "I want everything with you, Mister Cruze."

The sharpness in his gaze softens into understanding and love, but there's a hint of flirtatious teasing in his reply. "And I want everything with you, Mister Masters."

Zephyr punctuates the sentiment by gripping my ass firmly and pulling me tightly against his body, where I can feel his growing arousal against mine.

He backs me up until I feel the mattress of the bed against the backs of my knees, and then, with a smirk, he shoves me backwards and I land with an amused *'oomph'*.

"I'm gonna take good care of you, Ted," he declares, prowling over my prone form with the grace of a mountain lion (or the professional dancer that he is). His hands work quickly to divest me of my clothes and he sucks and licks wet kisses over every inch of skin that he reveals as he goes.

I've never done this before. Not just bottoming, but letting my lover take complete control of the situation. But with Zephyr it's okay. It's right. This is the man who still takes me over his lap and metes out spankings that I never before knew I needed. This is the man who showed me that it's okay not to be okay. This is the man who never once pushed me beyond my limits, but wouldn't let me hide behind a false façade, either. The man who watched me fall apart and, instead of running away, stood by my side and helped me as I worked to put myself back together — properly this time.

As he brings lubed fingers to my hole and massages my rim slowly and patiently, murmuring praise and reassurances when he finally works one of his long, slender digits inside me, I'm once again reminded that he's not like any other Little I've been with before.

In fact, right now, there's no sign of that part of him at all. Even though he's never topped before, he's all confidence and self-assurance. He's the embodiment of strength and passion. He's the caregiver right now, and I'm his to take care of. And fuck but it feels good to let go and let him do this.

At his urging, I spread my legs wider and I can't describe the sound I make when one finger becomes two and then three. I get even louder and more insistent when he curls them and, after a few moments of searching, finds that spot inside me which makes me see stars.

Yes, the stretch and the burn is uncomfortable, but it gives way to pleasure the more Zephyr grazes over my prostate again…and again…*and again.* My cock is aching and leaking pre-cum, but neither one of us reaches for it. I don't want to risk coming until he's inside me. I want him to feel me squeezing around him when I finally go over the edge.

I'm babbling incoherently by the time he finally deems me ready for his cock. I can't even tell you when he undressed, but when I open my eyes to complain that he's removed his fingers, he's naked and stroking himself with lube, his gorgeous dark skin glinting gold under the hotel room's warm lighting.

He's an absolute vision.

And he's mine.

"*Zeph*," his name falls from my lips on a moan, "kitten, you're so fucking hot…"

"I can't promise I'll last long," he says apologetically, sliding his hands under my thighs to manhandle me into position.

With the leaking head of his cock nudging my hole, I shake my head emphatically. "I don't care. I almost came from your fingering. I— *unnnngh…*" The wanton sound is forced from me as he slides inside me with one long, slow push of his hips.

The burn is greater than his fingers had been, and he makes shushing sounds, sliding his palms over my sweat-slicked thighs which tremble around his hips. He doesn't move, waiting for me to acclimate. My beautiful, perfect, considerate boy.

"*Ted*," he groans, "you're…this is…you feel…I…thank you. Jesus, fuck," he gasps. "*Fuck*, I love you."

His rambled words help me to relax against the intrusion of his cock inside me, and I can briefly imagine how overwhelmed he probably feels right now, too. The tight, slick heat that surrounds him. The emotional connection between us. The insane amount of trust we've given each other over the past few months. I feel that way every time I sink inside his young, lithe body, too. But the first time? That's intense all on its own.

"I love you too, kitten," I pant through the last twinges of pain, experimentally rocking my hips and feeling the sparks of pleasure flaring in its place, "now, baby, move. Please."

He doesn't need to be asked twice. As if by some unspoken agreement, we're both content to take it slowly. Zephyr is gentle but purposeful with every roll of his hips, and the praises and commentary he's murmuring are equal parts arousing and endearing.

"Oh, shit, fuck…Ted…*Daddy*…I'm so close," he eventually declares, stretching out over me to bring our mouths together in a sloppy, strung-out, desperate kiss. His hand finds my cock and starts to fist it with his thrusts. "You…you feel…"

He swivels his hips and I cry out, my hands scrabbling for purchase in the sheets beneath me as he finds my prostate again.

"There?" he asks, repeating the motion without waiting for my answer.

Between his hand milking me and his dick suddenly moving with precision, I'm a whimpering, blathering mess when I erupt between us, seeing stars. I barely register Zephyr's hips stilling or his babbled stream of "Daddy, *Daddy*, oh, oh fuck, I'm co…*Daddy*, oh fuck, *fuuuuuuck*" as his cock pulses jet after jet of his passion inside me.

My heart is still pounding as my boy carefully pulls out and then collapses on top of me, smearing my cum over both our bodies.

I'm sated and boneless and feel lighter than air. My thoughts are a jumble of happiness and hopes for a future that suddenly looks even brighter than before. It's funny how an orgasm can do that.

Closing my eyes and catching my breath, I rest my chin on top of Zephyr's head where it's pillowed on my chest. I'm still amazed at how much has changed in such a short time. When we met, I couldn't have predicted the path our relationship would take.

If anything, I thought we'd have a little bit of fun and part ways as friends. Now, I can't imagine not having him in my life at all. I feel complete. Whole again, after a lifetime of living in barely fused together pieces.

And all of that can be attributed to the man in my arms now.

I never thought I'd find a life partner or a Forever Little, especially not at my best friend's wedding, but if I had the chance to do it all over again…even all the hard stuff?

I wouldn't change a thing.

The End

* * *

Thank you so much for reading *Ted's Temerity*. I genuinely hope you liked it as much as I enjoyed writing it. Ted's backstory threw me for a loop when I first started writing this one, and I *may* have sat and cried over my laptop a lot while the first draft came together. But I think his and Zephyr's Happily Ever After has come out well in the end.

Anyway, I'd love it if you could leave a review on Amazon or on Goodreads. Reviews not only tell the algorithms that our books deserve attention, but honest feedback also encourages and inspires me to keep writing. Even a star rating helps, and I greatly appreciate you making time to do so.

Speaking of my writing: if you're still enjoying the antics of the *Littles & Lace* crew, keep turning the pages for a sneak peek of Book 4 titled *Spencer's Satisfaction*.

And, if you'd like a free ebook copy of *Charlie's Contentment* (a 10,000 word zero-angst, high-fluff novella which functions as an extended epilogue for *Asher's Answer,* but can also be read as a super sweet stand-alone) subscribe to my newsletter here:

https://annasparrows.com/newsletter-subscription/

For updates, release dates, competitions and more, follow me on Facebook. The link is in the 'About The Author' page after the sneak peek.

Sneak Peek – Spencer's Satisfaction

Chapter One – Spencer

"And that's a wrap," Becky, the studio engineer and producer I've been recording with for the last couple of days declares cheerfully from behind plexiglass. "I think that was a record, Spence."

I pull off my headphones and give my wild hair a shake out, stretching my neck and grinning back at her. We've worked together on a few projects now, and it's starting to show. We're like a well-oiled machine at this rate.

"Not many bloopers this time around," I acknowledge, chuckling. "Should we stage a few for J.C.? I hear some authors are sharing our fuckups as bonus content these days."

I leave the booth and meet her outside the door.

"Whatever sells the books, babe," Becky shrugs, before her plump lips pull into a smirk, "and you still gave me plenty to work with on that front, don't worry. I mean, yesterday you completely forgot to switch your voice into Melody's for the sex scene, remember?"

I cringe. "Ugh. Rookie error for sure. I still blame you for making me record that one first up before I had enough caffeine in my system."

She cackles like a 1960s *Batman* villain, throwing her head back, making her long dark hair sway with the movement. "It. Was. Gold." She proceeds to deepen her voice into a mockery of mine as she re-enacts some of the scene in question.

"Shut up," I huff, then frown and point my index finger at her for good measure, "that shit could be taken as transphobic. Maybe in my creative interpretation of Melody's character, she's MTF. Who are you to judge?"

"She got pregnant in the first scene you recorded, dumbass. Your logic is flawed."

I can't help snorting at that. With my hands held in surrender, I shrug. "All I'm saying is that there are women out there with deep voices, too."

Hell, most of my female characters are spoken in a softened version of my own voice. I don't buy in to the practice of pitching my voice comically higher. As a listener, I think it can come off condescending and cringe-worthy (not unlike a woman making her voice sound ridiculously deep to voice a male character, like Becky just did playfully).

She arches one of her eyebrows at me. "You're serious."

"I am." We haven't really ever shared any deep and meaningful discussions in our past interactions, so my reticence to come off even at all offensive or exclusionary might come as a surprise to her. Nevertheless, 'live and let live' is an adage I genuinely try to practice.

"Shit, Spence, I'm sorry. I just thought it was funny."

"No, no," I realize that I might have come on a little too strong with my ideologies, too, "it was. I mean, in context it was hilarious." We'd had tears rolling down our faces at the time. The re-take had also taken an hour longer than either of us had planned because one of us would inevitably start laughing again once the other had calmed down, setting the other off again. On a sigh, I add, "I'm just sensitive about these things. Y'know…inclusion. LGBTQ rights. The whole shebang."

And don't get me started on my 'Bi/Pan Erasure' rant. Bisexuality and pansexuality exist, damn it. But if I'm dating a woman, people assume I'm straight, and if I'm dating a man, they assume I'm gay, and God forbid I publicly flirt with both genders at the one event!

"Of course, babe. I'm sorry. I wasn't…I didn't mean…"

Crap. Now I feel bad. I honestly don't mean to talk *at* people like that. Or to lecture like that. Or to make people feel bad for just having a little fun. I don't. But, at the same time, I struggle to just let potentially offensive stuff go. I mean, in the right context there was nothing malicious about it, but what if someone had walked into the studio and misunderstood where it was coming from?

"No, I know; I'm sorry," I scrub a hand down my face and curse myself for having derailed the conversation so spectacularly.

Well done, Highland. Can't even carry on a conversation with a colleague…

Grimacing at the turn my thoughts have taken, I add, "I guess it's been a long day and I'm more tired than I thought."

Becky waves me off with a smile laced with understanding. "You're a good guy. It's nice that you think of other people's feelings."

"It's all that romance I read," I jest, trying to lighten the mood.

"It puts me in touch with my softer side or whatever."

"Uh huh." Becky doesn't sound convinced, but the smile toying at the edge of her lips is playful. She bumps my shoulder with hers. "I'm sure that's it."

I scoop up my satchel from the floor outside the booth and fiddle with the strap as I loop it over my shoulder. I'm always a little awkward with goodbyes, even professional ones.

"So," I say, aiming for casual despite the clusterfuck of the conversation we've just shared, "it was awesome working with you again. You'll call if anything needs to be re-recorded?"

Becky nods. "It was," she agrees, "and I will." She cocks her head to the side. "Rumor has it you've got yourself a home studio now. Do you do your own post-production?"

"Yeah. It's...*ugh.* Honestly, I hate doing it. But it keeps my overheads low and maximizes my profits, so..."

"I get it. If I could perform, I'd be set. But, trust me, *nobody* wants me reading their books." She sighs dramatically. "Turns out acting isn't in my wheelhouse."

"You could take lessons," I offer helpfully. "Performing for narration purposes isn't the same as acting – it's all vocal work, and you don't have to memorize anything." The face she makes has me chuckling and holding my hands up in the universal gesture of surrender. "Or not. It was just a suggestion."

"To be fair, my job keeps me busy enough. But the idea of starting my own company with the ability to work from home has its appeal."

As someone who took the plunge and invested in building a little studio in their basement, I wholeheartedly agree with her. I still take on jobs for publishing houses and established production companies but having my own space and being able to offer my services as a narrator or voice over artist under my own company name (and rates) has been incredibly liberating.

Becky and I walk together and continue our conversation as we leave the building which houses the recording studio and their offices and meander towards the parking lot. She asks me about how much it cost me to set my home studio up, and I happily give her all the information I have. She's not my direct competition, after all, and it's always nice to talk to someone else who understands the intricacies of my job.

The guys I'm closest to try their best, but I'm pretty sure they all think it's a walk in the park. After all, how hard can it be to be paid to read a script out loud with no physical audience? Harder than they think, I assure you.

After we say our goodbyes, I head home, smiling when I'm greeted at the door by my cat. He's a rescue from the local shelter, sleek and black and vocal as fuck.

"Hey, Frank," I greet him, earning myself a loud, drawn-out *'mrrrrow'* in return. He winds around my ankles, butting his head into my shin. "I missed you too, bud."

After dropping my satchel on the side table in the entryway, I reach down to stroke my hand over his back, smiling as I always do when he arches up off the floor for more, purring deep and loudly.

"At least I can get *someone's* engine running," I mutter to myself as the rumbling sound starts up.

Frank twists around with that effortless grace gifted to all felines and nudges my hand for more pets. "Alright, alright, you attention whore," I grumble lightheartedly, picking him up and cradling him against my chest. His purr vibrates against me, soothing away the remaining stresses of my day.

My friend Chance (probably my closest friend, considering I hang out with him more than any of the other guys in our social circle, especially since they've all started finding partners to settle down with) gave me no end of grief when I first adopted Frank.

"Cats are assholes," he'd said, trying to convince me to get a dog instead. "They're selfish and aloof and not at all affectionate. And they break shit. Like, on purpose. They look you dead in the eye and do it. I've seen it on YouTube."

I'd argued that cats are generally cleaner, more willing to entertain themselves when I'm out at work, and I've never had to strap a leash to a cat and walk it for hours on end. Cats also don't cause noise disturbance for the neighbors or during my recording sessions. As much as I also love dogs, a cat was a better fit for my lifestyle at the time (and still is). Plus, Frank had totally proven Chance wrong when it came to how affectionate he was when I first saw him.

And, yeah, the fact that Emma, my ex, had also loved cats had been a draw card, too.

I'm just glad she didn't fight me for custody. I wouldn't have gotten through the last couple of years without my furry little companion.

Frank meows again as I walk towards the kitchen. He's got our routine memorized at this point, and he knows that his dinner is about to be served. I talk to him about my day as I pull out a can of gourmet cat food (shut up, he's fussy) and then set him down on the tiled kitchen floor in front of his food and water bowls.

He eats his meal while I reheat myself some leftover Chinese food from last night and then perches himself on the armrest of the couch as I settle in to eat and watch TV, occasionally reaching out a soft black paw (complete with the cutest pink toe-beans) in an attempt to steal from my fork as it moves towards my mouth. And if I give in and hand feed him little bits of braised chicken, nobody else is any the wiser.

'You're spending another Friday night alone with your pussy again, aren't you?' Chance's text message comes through midway through my attempt to catch up on the last season of *The Great British Bake Off.*

I roll my eyes and text back, *'For a gay man, you're kind of obsessed with what I do with pussy.'*

'I take that as 'Yes, Chance, I am channeling my inner old lady again'. You're not fooling anyone by deflecting.'

I snort. He knows me too well. *'You got me. All I need is a pair of knitting needles and I could be someone's grandma.'*

'Come out to The Grove tonight.' He replies, cutting to the chase. I groan. Before I can respond, he adds, *'Please?'*

I'm pretty sure he knows I'm going to give in even before I send my response. *'Fine. But you're buying the drinks.'*

About the Author

I've been writing* for as long as I can remember. I started with silly short stories as a kid, moved on to fanfiction in my teens (and still write it now), and am also a published MF romance author under a second pen name.

I have been an avid reader of MM romance my whole life. (Ask me about my beginnings with *Buffy* fanfic, haha.) I wrote a sweet and kinky MM romance novel in 2022 and the reader response changed my life. From there, I knew I had found my niche.

And thus Anna Sparrows was born.

*All of my writing is 100% my own. No part of it is generated by Artificial Intelligence (AI) software of any kind. Yes, that means that it's sometimes flawed, but I'm okay with that.

You can connect with me on:

- https://annasparrows.com
- https://www.facebook.com/AnnaSparrowsAuthor
- https://www.instagram.com/annasparrows

Subscribe to my newsletter:

- https://annasparrows.com/newsletter-subscription

Also by Anna Sparrows

I write ridiculously sweet & steamy MM romance with guaranteed HEAs…and sometimes with a side of kink.

Littles & Lace Series
The Littles & Lace series is an MM Age Play series, following a group of like-minded friends in the BDSM community. You'll find mild ABDL, light Pet Play, Femme Play and more here.

Book 1: Asher's Answer

Book 2: Matteo's Mettle

Book 3: Ted's Temerity

Book 4: Spencer's Satisfaction

Book 5: Chance's Choice

Book 6: Josh's Jackpot

Dads & Adages Series

Visit Australia's sunny Gold Coast where an assortment of single dads find love and even learn a few life lessons along the way.

Book 1: Where There's A Will

Book 2: You Don't Know Jack

Book 3: A Match Made In Evan (release TBA)

Shifters Sanctuary Series

In a world where alphas are thought to be extinct, a number of 'human' men are about to have their worlds rocked.

Book 1: His Alpha Unlocked

Book 2: His Prodigal Alpha (release TBA)

www.ingramcontent.com/pod-product-compliance
Lightning Source LLC
Chambersburg PA
CBHW070609120726
47909CB00007B/2497